Accolades for *Land of the Cranes*

2021 Américas Award Winner

2020 Jane Addams Children's Book Honor Award
for Older Children

2021 Northern California Book Award Winner

2021 California Library Association's
Beatty Award Winner

2021 International Latino Book Awards
Silver Medal—Best Youth Latino Focused
Chapter Book

2021 Charlotte Huck Honor Award for Outstanding
Fiction for Children

New York Public Library's Best Books of 2020

SLJ Best Books of 2020

2021 Project LIT Book Club Pick

2021 Rise: A Feminist Book Project List

2021 Children's Book Committee,
Bank Street College of Education Best
Children's Books of the Year

2022 Rhode Island Latino Book
Awards Reading List

2020 Vermont Golden Dome Book List

A Best Book of 2020 by the Center for the
Study of Multicultural Children's Literature

A Best Book of 2020 by *Kirkus Reviews*

A Best Book of 2020 by *BookPage*

Starred Reviews from *Kirkus Reviews,*
Publishers Weekly, and *School Library Journal*

Praise for *The Moon Within*

★ "A worthy successor to *Are You There God? It's Me, Margaret* set in present-day Oakland . . . Salazar's verse novel is sensitive and fresh."
—*Kirkus Reviews*, starred review

"With conga-pulsed lyrics, Aida Salazar pulls us into the coming of age of eleven year Celi. She initiates readers into the conversation of Bomba, the girl-woman circle, divine twin energies and the many moon-tide powers of a Latina pre-teen. This is a book whose form and content, vision and depth, I find revolutionary and culturally ecstatic. In these times, here is the liberation verse our youth and all have been waiting for—Brava-Bravo!" —Juan Felipe Herrera, former US Poet Laureate and author of *Jabberwalking*

"Aida Salazar has reached deep into our indigenous past to explore in beautiful, poignant poetry what it means to become a woman at the intersection of community and self. Rooted in ancestral lore yet vibrantly modern, *The Moon Within* is a touching, powerful, and important novel in verse."
—David Bowles, Pura Belpré
Honor-winning author of *They Call Me Güero*

"In a vivid, magical debut, Aida Salazar's lyrical poetry deftly pulls you into Celi's vibrant world as she reluctantly dances towards womanhood, adjusting to the drumbeats of first love and true friendship while exploring her ancestral roots as she finds her role within family and community." —Naheed H. Senzai, award-winning author of *Shooting Kabul* and *Escape from Aleppo*

LAND OF THE CRANES

BY AIDA SALAZAR

Scholastic Inc.

Interior illustrations © 2020 by Quang & Lien
Text copyright © 2020 by Aida Salazar

This book was originally published in hardcover by Scholastic Press in 2020.

ISBN 978-1-338-34386-1

10 9 8 7 6 5 4 3 2   23 24 25 26

Printed in the U.S.A.   40
This edition first printing 2022
Book design by Maeve Norton

For my bella Mami,
Maria Isabel Viramontes Salazar,
in her eternal flight

My papi says,
Long ago, our people came from a place
called Aztlán, the land of the cranes
which is now known as the Southwestern US.
They left Aztlán to fulfill their prophecy:
to build a great city
in the navel of the universe
a small mound in the middle of a lake
where they saw an eagle devour a serpent on a cactus.
They called that place Mexica-Tenochtitlán.
It was also prophesized
our people would return to Aztlán
to live among the cranes again.

Aztlán

A SOFT MEMORY

I don't remember the mountain
        where I was born
or the place where I first crawled.

I remember Mami's worried mouth
a whisper that she, Papi, and I
        would follow
a flock of cranes going
home
        El Norte, Los Angeles.

There, we could be birds too—brown grullas
where bad men could not harm us
like they did my Tío Pedro
and Abuelita would not worry.

Seven years later
I think I remember the soft wrinkles
on Abuelita Lola's face.

WHAT I KNOW:

I know my school's shiny floors
a broken water fountain
and boxed chocolate milk
I buy for fifty cents.

I know Ms. Martinez
        and her
happy handshakes
        at her door
before each fourth-grade morning.

I know how to write
and draw the picture poems
Ms. Martinez taught us
to paint our feelings.

I know to never forget
to scribble my name and date
on the bottom.

I know recess on the blacktop
and the length of my golden
brown crane wings
in the desert sun.

I know my BFF, Amparo
climbs los columpios like wind.

I know aftercare until six p.m.
when Papi comes to get me
        between
                his two jobs
and carries me home
                on his
strong shoulders
                so high I find
                        flight.

HOW I LEARNED TO FLY

Blue   sky   flight
began
with a   ripple
of feathers
tickled   by air
on the surface
     of my dancing arms.

Sprouting wings stumbled
     with the wind
pushed sideways
     at first
I heard
Papi's voice,

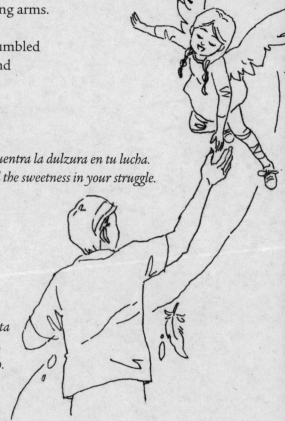

     Encuentra la dulzura en tu lucha.
     Find the sweetness in your struggle.

Then, a breath
a thought
to spell
my smiling name
with my wings
big circles to form
     Roberta, Betita
my name like Papi's
     Roberto, Beto.

Then, a glide
a laugh so loud

looked down to see
las casas, las yardas,
and barking dogs
of our vecindad
become tiny
dots and squares
as I floated
above
      with Papi flying beside me
          ready to catch me
              all the way home.

WHERE WE LAND

Papi and I land
on the front yarda
of our duplex
each day.

He shuffles in his pocket
for the keys to our rental
        and in we go
to our one-bedroom casita
plus the laundry room
he turned
into a mini bedroom
with all-year Xmas lights
        for me.

He puts down his so heavy
worker's belt inside his cool gray
toolbox and fires up the comal.
We sit to eat beans and tortillas,
chile, with a sprinkle of cheese.

This is when he tells me
old stories about how we come
        from the
                people of the sun
        and how long ago
                we lived in Aztlán
        among the cranes
                and danced

and crooned like trumpets
            about how we left
and built our great city
            in the belly button of the universe.
He talks with cheeks full of food
from the side of his mouth,
The prophecy says
            one day
    we will fly back home
            and croon, cry, and build
    our nests in the place
            we once left.

He says all of us cranes
are giving the prophecy life.

Then, he goes to curl into a nap
for half an hour while I fly
outside to play
            with Amparo
in the tree-filled yarda
we share with her family
            until
brown feathered-skin Mami
            comes home
sometimes with
a bag of bright yellow lemons
like a gift in her tired hands
singing
            a sweet song in Spanish
a swing
            from her lips

and we crowd into
      one another
      with kisses
      and hugs
and how-was-your-days
      before Papi rushes off
to dip his hands
      in suds
to make restaurant dishes
      clean.

CRANE POEM GALLERY

Before his nap today
Papi asks to see
my daily picture poem.
I pull it out from my backpack
and uncrumple the edges.
What marvel did you make today, Betita?
he asks in his Spanish-sounding English
       warm soft round words
             are air to me
but so strange to others they call it an accent
different, a little, from my own singsong East LA English
Principal Brown tries
to correct
but Ms. Martinez
never cared
       one speck
           about.

Papi smoothes the edges
raises the paper up to the light
to inspect it like an X-ray
studying first the drawing
with a wheel-like twist of his mouth.
He sees:
       me perched up on the rocket tower
       of our jungle gym at school
       my eyes closed
       wings out to my sides
       the wind drawing

a wide grin across my face.
Then he reads the rhyming poem I scribbled below my picture:

Recess

Running, sliding, climbing to reach the sky
up so high, I almost fly.

He traces my signature with his finger.
It's my best new cursive:

Betita–September 7

He kisses his pride right onto
my cheek with an extra-loving push
that makes my head wobble.
You sign just like an artist, mi Plumita.
I thought maybe like a poet, Papi, I say
because Ms. Martinez just taught us about
Juan Felipe Herrera, the poet of the nation
who is a crane like us.
Yes, like a poet too, amor.

I watch him hang
my crane poem
on what Mami calls
my "laundry line gallery"
she strung up across
the kitchen window
above the sink
while she whistled.

WE PLANTED ROSES TOO

Papi planted trees
along the square edges
of our wrought iron fence
to leave some grass
in the middle
for Amparo and me
to run and for our families
to gather and
grill carne asada
on the weekend.

He planted
        guamúchil
        guayaba
        chabacano
        and plum
pruned trees
ripe with fruit
perfect branches
the best for climbing.

Then, Mami said,
Quiero rosas for my altar, por favor.
        So, all of our hands planted
bald bushes at first
with knots for roots
that later burst into
bold green leaves
with big red flowers

carrying a smell so sweet
summer wind circles
the sugary air across
the yarda and through
our windows
and into
our noses
and into
an
ahh.

VIRGENCITA ANGEL

Mami lights a candle daily
to a small statue of La Virgen de Guadalupe
and a picture of Tío Pedro faded in a frame.

His whole face is a smile.
His big wavy hair is like Mami's
        but shorter
and he's got a reddish-brown
hair donut around his mouth
Mami doesn't have
except for one whisker
that grows under her chin.

Can I light the match? Por please?
Con cuidado not to get burned, hijita.

She prays for protection under her breath
while she fusses with the roses
in the vase and the little milagrito
metal charms of hands and hearts
scattered at La Virgencita's feet.

As I stare at Mami's altar
I notice each time, we are
the brown of this Virgen
the morena of her
painted ceramic skin.

I spot the slice of moon
and the winged angel
that holds her up.
My favorite part.
I smile to think maybe
La Virgencita is a bird.

Virgencita llena eres de gracia . . .

Mami, excuse me, but I think . . .

. . . protégenos con tu manto.

La Virgencita has wings
like her baby angel.

Mami giggles
and pokes my panza.
Maybe she is hiding them in her robes!
Or behind her arms!
Our giggles tumble together
under La Virgencita's patient eyes.

Mami. Is Tío Pedro with her?

Mami's smile melts.
She nods her head a little
and stares into her brother's picture.

Yes, mi'ja. He is with her now.

I SPELL A SPELL

Ms. Martinez teaches me magic.

She casts the vocabulary words
all fourth graders should know
onto the white board
for us to squeeze into memory.
        The funnest game.

I love to loop and lift
the lines to make shapes
mean something
on my paper.

Words in English
I don't know at first
but the more I draw the curves
and lines, then hear the way they
sound out loud, the more alive
they are in my head.

Words like:
        intonation   or   fortune
        energy   or   angle
        anguish   or   freedom
        myth   or   alchemy
are the almost spells
I spell
with ink.

JELLY RANCHERA STRIDES

From my cushy bed
Saturday-morning sounds
     are a blast of rancheras
swooshing into our house
     leftover music from
Omar's ritual car wash
     and el paletero's bell
ring,   ring,   ringing
     and Papi's calling,
¡Para arriba, Betita Plumita!
Los quince de Tina are today!

I squeeze my ojos shut
     but my ears are two nets
snatching more sounds
     the tiny cackle of Amparo's baby brother
and the fart noises I know she makes
     by catching air in her armpits
make me giggle
     before Papi tickles my toes really awake.

I tumble out of my blankets
     follow the smell of huevitos
and café coming from the kitchen
     thinking about
my cousin Tina's
     round yellow dress.

I run into Papi
        spin,   spin,   spinning
Mami away from the stove
        he tucks her into a cheek-to-cheek
two-step ranchera
        then pulls me
into a close snug.
        I bury my face
into Mami's squishy belly
        feeling my mouth   stretch
into the sappiest jelly grin
        as I bounce
along to their
        two-step ranchera strides.

SANCTUARY BREAKFAST

When we sit to eat
I bring my paper and crayons.
Guarda eso, Betita, focus on eating.
Mami slides me my dish.
With a wink from Papi
I drift into my drawing.

> Tina in her quince dress
> her straight blue-black hair
> that I use two colors to get just right.
> I draw myself in my new
> dusty-rose dress
> holding her hand
> my mouth so open
> a fly is about to go inside.

Six raids in the last two days, Papi chews.

> *Where?*

In the factories just over the tracks.
People say there will be more.
This administration is out to get us.

> *But this is a sanctuary state.*

> A what, Mami?

Papi clears his throat and
almost whispers,
A "sanctuary" is a place where cranes can't get caught.

      Caught for doing what?

They look at each other
and then at me.
I can tell I'm not supposed to ask
by the way their worried eyebrows
push down
on their blabber-mouth eyes.

For just wanting to fly, Plumita.

      So can we get caught too?

Betita, Mami quiets me, *eat up, cielito.*
We have to get to church early
before the ceremony. Mira, look
at this beautiful bouquet I made from
our rosales for Tina to offer La Virgen.

I look down without their answer
and quickly draw a bouquet of flowers
in Tina's other hand.
The only wordspell I have time to cast
is my curly name and the date
on the bottom.
Betita–September 15

LOS QUINCE DE TINA

I looove Tina's fancy dress
big and bouncy golden-yellow satin
with sparkly flowers at the hem.

Her fanciness courtesy of
Mami and Papi
the padrinos of that dress
'cause they paid for all
but the last one hundred dollars
Tina's dad, Tío Juan, threw in.

Tío Juan is Papi's brother
and the first crane to fly here
a long time ago.
He helped Papi find a job in
construction, and Tía Raquel,
Tina's mamá, helped Mami
find work taking care of babies.

They are part of the flock we have here.

Tina shows me her Gram page
with all the facial tutorials
she likes and uses *me*
to test them out.
Then we take pictures and videos of our
slathered green avocado faces
and cucumber eyes
she posts to her Gram story

and we wait for the likes to pop in
from her almost one thousand followers!

Funny to think what she might look like
in an oatmeal mask and poofy sparkly dress.

But right now our happiness
is big and wide because she looks like Belle
dancing a waltz with gruff Tío Juan
in her *Beauty and the Beast* backyard ballroom.
Paper flowers all around the tall rented canopy
yellow ribbons woven into the chain-link fence.

Tía Raquel stops her running around
long enough to get weepy happy
and wipe her tears with the
corner of her plaid apron
over her lacy navy dress.

A bunch of Tina's school friends
are here wearing so much makeup
and tiny dresses so tight, they look really old
like grown-up old.

Tío Desiderio is on guard
at the bar, making sure some
of her pimply-faced guy friends
don't try to get beer.

Most of the smaller kids
are weaving in and out of tables
between the older tíos and tías sitting
on folding chairs and fanning themselves
because of the late-summer heat, but not me.
My eyes are drinking up Tina
floating
       and
            gliding
like a dancing crane.

I tug on Mami's
dress and point at Tina and
then right back at me.

One day, I wish to have a
backyard *Beauty and the Beast*
ballroom crane quince
like Tina.

By the way Mami squeezes
my round cheeks
with her manicured fingers
      I think she wants one for me too.

CARTEL

At aftercare pickup
Papi says,
Now that you are a fourth grader
it's time for you to know
the meaning of the word
"cartel" in Spanish.

"Cartel," a cardboard sign
to announce something
as in "for sale"
or "car wash here."
But also,
a group of men who sell
       drugs
       guns
       and people
       sometimes.

A cartel hurt Tío Pedro
made him disappear
when he didn't give them
the money they wanted
and then, wanted to come
for us too
though we had nothing
to do with it.

It's why we can't see
Abuelita Lola anymore.

We were lucky Tío Juan
petitioned for us
to be here before we knew
of cartels.
      Petition?
It's like getting on a wait list.
      For what?
To fly free, Plumita.

When I ask Papi
if the men in cartels
are cranes like us
he says,
It's impossible, Betita
because their souls
are so mangled
they have forgotten
how to be birds.

THE AMPARO GLOBE

In Ms. Martinez's class
Amparo invites me to play
a mapping game on a globe.
She tilts her round head
and her floppy ponytail whips
to the side when she asks.

I am always ready
to play with Amparo.

She explains,
Okay, Betita,
first I'll find a random place
then I'll spin the globe
and you have to find it.
Ready . . .   *Madagascar!*

I find it easy.
      Here!
      This big island floating
      in the sea next
      to Africa.

When we switch
      I run my fingers over
the bumps on the globe
      that mean mountains
and continents
      and make my fingers dance.

I start at Alaska
    and feel the ridges
        run into the Rocky Mountains
            then turn into the Sierra Madres
                the bumpy mountains connected
            like a curvy spine
        all the way down
      the back of North America.

These are all the places
Papi said cranes fly.

Amparo snaps,
C'mon, Betita, give me a place!

Without looking I say,
      Here, find Aztlán
      and spin.

She squeezes
her hazel eyes
almost closed at me.
She knows it's a trick question
but she goes along.

Ay, your papi says Aztlán
doesn't exist in real life anymore.
That the Aztecs left it a long time ago.

      Yes it DOES exist, tell me
      where is it now?

She rolls her eyes but answers,
Okay, we are rebuilding it here in East LA.
Amparo points to LA on the globe
then she places her hand over
her chest and says,
También in here.

I get cartwheel happy
because Amparo
has been listening
to Papi's stories!
She knows
she is a crane too!

WAITING

On Monday
Papi must be late. It's six p.m.
and aftercare closes at six fifteen.
The ticks on the clock
are honey-slow tocks
I try not to count.
I wonder if Papi's broken a wing
on the skyscrapers he helps build
with hammers and steel?

I wonder if Papi forgot
I am waiting and rushed
to the restaurant with too
many dishes to wash?

But that has never happened.

Ms. Cassandra, the teacher's aide,
bends the creases of her forehead
near her phone when Papi doesn't answer.
So she calls Mami, who is the nanny
of toddler twins with bright red cheeks
who can't fly.

Ms. Cassandra gives me a tissue
to soak up my teariness because Mami
can't come for me right now either.

She can't leave those babies
until *their* parents get home.

Papi is coming, I whisper to myself.

I'll tuck my wings close and wait.

6:15 P.M.

When the hand of the clock
is past six fifteen and there is no Papi
the sun is still so bright outside.
Principal Brown drives me
to Mami's work
as far away as forever from school
though close to where
Principal Brown lives.

She tells me,
Everything will be okay, Betita.
Your father probably got caught up.

I'm not sure.

I want Papi.

THE BIG HOUSE

Where Mami works is so big
it could be a scraper Papi built.

As we arrive, Mami is closing
the wide wood front door behind her.
She wraps one arm around me.
Betita, nada pasa. Todo está bien.
Her face doesn't match her words.
Something *is* happening, and it *isn't* okay.
I don't get to see inside.
I don't get to meet the twins.
I don't get to see how
those who aren't cranes live.

Thank you, Principal Brown. Mami's voice breaks.

*You're welcome. Please let me know
if there is anything else I can do,*
she tells Mami.

We walk to the bus stop
and watch Principal Brown drive off.
Mami is on the phone
now a faucet of drip-drop
tears falling on the pavement.
When I ask her what happened to Papi
she shakes her head
as if to say,
Not now, Betita.

From a string
of weeping words
I learn
someone named ICE
put Papi and other hammer workers
        in a cage
and Mami doesn't know
how to set him free.

I cry to think of Papi
unable to fly.

WALLS

On the bus, Mami says
here in El Norte
there are walls we were not
supposed to cross.

We are sin papeles
   undocumented, her voice trembles.
A word that means
"without permission."

I remind Mami this is
the land of the cranes.
We have wings
that can soar above walls.

Sí, mi amor, but not
when they have cages
and can stop us from flying.

She sweeps me into
a one-handed hug and
kisses the top of my head.
I watch the traffic turn
from smooth to crowded
through the window of the bus
taking us home.

A PAPI IN A PILLOW

That night
I crawl into Mami and Papi's bed
smell for Papi on his pillow.

I stare at Mama's Virgen altar.
Will I ever see him again?

I take scissors and cut out a square
from his baby-blue pillowcase
tuck the cloth into my blouse
and secure it with a safety pin
near my heart.

I cut out another little piece
and put it on Mami's Virgencita
smoosh it between the moon
and the angel
and pray for protection.

> Please, Virgencita, don't
> take Papi with you too.

Mami is in the living room
with Amparo's mom, Diana.
They are two cranes murmuring.

She arranges for Diana
to get me after school
until Mami comes for me
at their casita just next door.

Diana will never be able to carry
Amparo
her baby
and me
on her
tiny
shoulders.

Could I fly without Papi?

NO ONE PUTS UP

my crane poem
the one about
a poet bird, Juan Felipe
the one signed and dated
     Betita–September 17

QUESTIONS

Ms. Martinez's handshake is
warmer than yesterday's.
She holds my hands between
hers like an empanada
in an oven
and blinks her small lashes.

Do you have any questions, Betita?

Before I can cry, I ask:
>Why would ICE take my papi?
>He only works.
>Hurts nobody.
>Will they make him go back
>to the mountain where
>mean men can hurt him?
>Back to an Abuelita Lola
>whose soft wrinkles
>we aren't supposed to know?

She hugs me and answers,
They might, sweet Betita.
Those who make laws don't care
how much your father gives.
Their laws are not always fair.
But there are others who might help him.
They are fighting for all those who migrate.

TWO DAYS

Two days since I've seen Papi's smile.
My own smile hides beneath my sadness.

So, I tug the cut pillow cloth
                    up
                to my nose
            and smell
the trace
of his feathers
in the cotton.

40

OUR FLOCK

Mami tells our flock
after three days they finally found
where they are keeping Papi.

Tía Raquel brings us
caldo de verduras and tortillas
            enough for the whole week.
Tío Juan brings us
people in suits
(lawyers, they call them)
who remind me of Ms. Martinez
with the way they speak
Spanish to Mami
English to themselves
though Mami can speak both.
I only catch one of their names . . .   Fernanda.

I don't understand
so many words.
"Petition,"   "failed to appear,"   "political asylum,"   "deportation"
only that Papi will be
put on a plane and flown
to Mexico.

Papi will not be able to
come back to us
for ten years, if he is lucky.

Fernanda explains,
He failed to appear in court
to have his petition heard.
It calls for immediate deportation.
            But he didn't receive notice!
Mami's explanation collapses like
the crushed tissue in her hand.
            What about ours?
Yours is still current but I will
also file for political asylum.
There is no telling how long it will take
or if your case will be approved at all.

Or, we could go
meet him in Mexico
a place too dangerous
to call home.

Time is slipping.
Mami has to decide.
She cups her hands
over her tummy
and lowers her face
to the ground.

Our flock huddles around Mami
touches the brown tips
of their wings together
and holds her
while she cries.

BROWN CRANE = TOCUILCOYOTL

Papi once told me,
The Nahuatl name for brown cranes is tocuilcoyotl.
Some lighter cranes cover their feathers
with mud to hide from predators while nesting.

I want to run out
to our yarda
and make a mud pile
so big
there is
enough
to cover
our entire
duplex
from
the
world.

A MUDDY NEST

Mami sends me to school
with Diana and Amparo.
She has been sick
in the bathroom
all morning.

A rope of knots
turned in my panza too
when I helped Mami
to bed
before I left.

As I walk, I wonder
if the plane Papi was on
        flew higher
than the travel paths
        of birds.

I wonder if Papi
        is with Abuelita Lola yet
though we aren't
even supposed to call
her on the phone
because they might
        find us.

I wonder if he was allowed
to take his hammers with him
to help him fight

if the cartel
        comes for him.

I wonder if he's hiding
        in the mountain
in a nest
        built of mud.

I wish we were
with Papi
and I didn't
have a Mami
so sad, she's sick
and alone
in bed.

EGG

Diana says,
*Be patient with your mami. On top of everything else
the new baby she's carrying is turning her upside down.*
            A baby, our own egg?
            Why didn't she tell me?
Oh! I'm sorry, Betita. I thought you knew.
I shake my head and bite my lower lip.
*Maybe 'cause she didn't want to worry you.
It'll be okay, Betita. She'll feel better in a month or two.*

I don't understand
why Mami and Papi
keep things from me.

*Hey, it's good to be an older sister!
Babies are squishy all over and they
giggle when you act goofy.*
Amparo opens her eyes wide.
But then, I don't hear Amparo anymore
because I think about the color
of the shell around Mami's baby
inside the nest of her body.

I worry because now we have
another thing to hide.

I worry.
How will we ever move a wounded nest?

LEARNING TEARS

Ms. Martinez calls us
into a circle at the reading carpet
and Principal Brown is there too
and so are some people
in fancy clothes
called social workers.

It turns out ICE stands for
            Immigration and Customs Enforcement.
They are the ones doing "round-ups"
collecting birds in cages
clipping their wings
and sending them back
to where they were born.

Ms. Martinez encourages us
to make a picture poem
or talk if we feel like it
or cry if that's what
turns inside us
            scared tears
            worried tears
            questioning tears
            crane tears
and we do.

They give us instructions:
*Make a family plan
in case someone in your*

family is rounded up
in a work raid.

There is no comfort in
what the fancy clothes say.

When Pepe raises his hand
to ask, *What about learning math today?*
Ms. Martinez looks at him
with eyes so heavy they looked closed.
We are learning about one another.
About the hurt in our hearts.
Sometimes, that is the most
important thing to learn.

I reach into my chest and softly
touch Papi's pillowcase square
that now begins to smell more
like my feathers
than his.

I want to go home
and put his pillowcase
            in a jar
so I can save the smell of Papi
until I can
            see him again.

I wish I knew
what Mami is going to do.

Will she make a plan for us?
Will we have to wait

all those years
or will we go
find him
hiding
in the
mountain?

PAPI IN A JAR

I decide to cut half
of Papi's pillowcase
and put it in a jar.

The other half I leave
on the pillow where
I now sleep with Mami
who is so sick
she can't take care of
the rosy-cheeked twins
this week.

Mami looks at the app
on her phone that tells
her how much money
we have in the bank.
          Our money is running out, she says.
She sings me a song
about a paraíso
with her sweet voice
before bed.

She cries into her
own pillow when
she thinks I am
asleep.

BROKEN WINGS

We finally hear from Papi!
Mami's hand shakes
so she hits speaker, sets it down
for both of us to hear.

I had to stay away
from the mountain, mi vida.
Se corre mucho peligro allí.
It is too dangerous there.

His voice is crashing
and crumbling
through the phone.

I'm in the big city, Guadalajara.
Are you okay, Papi?
I'm with other cranes with broken wings
but we help one another.

He says he is sleeping on the street
and looking for work
scraped together enough
just to make this call.

I want to know if he has a pillow.
He tells me,
It's okay, Betita.
I make one with my jacket.

I tell him about my pillow jar
and how I carry him everywhere.
He tells us about
his own secret money tin can
tucked in his cool gray toolbox
with money meant to surprise
Mami with a car.

Mami cries and promises
to put all of it in the bank
and send him some
so he can stop sleeping
on the street and so we
can come find him.

When Mami tells him
about the egg
she has in her nest
he cries too.
You've given me medicine
to heal what's broken in me.

Papi tells us he loves us
and says before he hangs up,
No matter how we struggle,
remember to keep life sweet.

SAFE

For the first time
in the two weeks
since they caged
my papi crane
       I smile.

DECISIONS

The next time
we speak
Papi's got
his own phone!
Papi and Mami
decide
it is best
for Mami
and the egg
and me
to stay until
it hatches
and grows a little.

Mami has lost
two babies before.
They worry this one
might get lost too.

Then, we can be
with Papi again.

Together.

CAJITA DE TESOROS

We make a plan with Diana
like Ms. Martinez and
Principal Brown said
            in case
            ICE ever
takes Mami at work
            and I am
                        left alone.

We make a box
of our treasures,
a cajita for Diana
to keep safe.
Mami calls our box
proof.

            Proof of what? I ask.

That we exist and
that we are good.

Mami shows me
and explains so I know too:
            our petition paperwork
            photos of us
            Abuelita Lola's phone number
            our bank card
            bills
            medical records

our filed taxes
pictures of what the mean men did to your Tío Pedro
you are not allowed to see
            and
this flash drive with
a digital copy of it all.
I add to the box of treasures
- the picture poem Papi never saw
- two jars:
        Papi's pillow jar
        and a new pillow jar
        I made
        from Mami's cut pillowcase.

Tío Juan and Tía Raquel
are on alert.
Diana now has keys.
She knows where
to find this cajita de tesoros
if the worst
ever happens.

WRITE ME!

Papi says he got the money
Mami sent him
*I'm not sleeping
on the street anymore!
I have my own pillow too
but my wings are still
a little bit injured.*

When I cry into
the phone he says,
*¡Escríbeme, Betita!
Write to tell me
how your day went—good or bad
or how good the chocolate milk is
or how to spell your favorite words
or how big the egg is getting, okei?
But leave your sadness there.
Remember la dulzura.*

I nod but he doesn't see me
through the phone.
¿Okei, mi Betita?

I will, Papi.
I'll send you
crane poems
every time
I want to
fly with you.

MAIL

The first one I send him:
I draw

>Mami and Papi's bed
>with smiley faces.

I write

>I sleep on your smiling pillow
>half of its case
>is missing like front teeth.
>Betita—October 9

SIX-MONTH SCIENTIST

I count six months till the egg
is supposed to hatch.
April.
Too long to wait to see Papi.

Maybe Papi will make his way
back to us before then?

Mami tells me,
Papi is looking for a job as an agrónomo.
             A what?
A plant and soil scientist.
             But Papi's a builder and a dishwasher, not a scientist?
That is what he was before we left Mexico.
He's interviewing for a job on an agave farm.
             Is it far away from the mountain?
Yes, Betita.
No one knows who he is there.

Papi's hammers won't
be needed on the farm.

I wonder what other
superpowers
my papi has
that I've never known?

A SONG

Mami is back with the twins.
She tells me she sings to them
       again
       like she used to do with me
       like she used to do
       when she was a teacher
       in Mexico.

We teach through song
because it makes learning fun and easier.
Who doesn't like a song?

It's true.
Mami learned the English
she knows by singing
pop songs on the radio.
She taught me
       my colors
       my shapes
       my numbers
       and multiplication
in Spanish
just that way
with her songs.

CRANE POEMS TO A FARM

I've stuck into my memory
the address to the farm
where Papi lives now
because I mail him
the picture poems
I promised
to keep life sweet.

I make them during aftercare
when I expect him
to walk in
      smile at me
           reach out his
                arms like ramps
                    ready to lift me up
but it is Diana
I see each day now.

I draw a heart
with wings
in the clouds
and the East LA
blue sky
with the words,
     Quiero volar
     en el cielo azul
     contigo, Papi.
     Betita–November 7

I draw a huge brown nest
with big eyes and long eyelashes
like Mami's
holding a tiny egg
and me sitting
crisscross applesauce
beside it
like I'm meditating
holding his pillow jar
in my hands
with the words:

> I wait
> for the
> baby crane
> to arrive
> and dream
> to see you again.
> Betita—December 12

COMMUNITY CORN

On a Saturday morning without Papi
Mami and I walk through
our vecindad to catch the bus
to the community clinic
for her checkup
with Sandra, the nurse midwife.
Then to church.

I practice flapping my feathers
while I trot to keep up to Mami.
The elotero walks fast
past us too, the bells of
his cart chiming into
our steps.
But we stop him
to buy an elote on a stick
dripping in mayo,
cheese, and chile.

Señoras wash and sweep
their concrete porches
yell at kids
to move their broken bikes
talk to one another
over their iron fences
hold their arms
in a fold above their panzas.

An old man in a vaquero hat
rides a bike with a plastic crate
strapped to his handlebars
holding a real live chicken.

Each house pushes out
its own smell
of homemade
          sopa or carnes or salsas
or the scent of
Pine-Sol mop water
emptied on a driveway.

But my favorite is the smell
of geraniums when
I snap a leaf and rub
it into my hands
          make one into a cup
up to Mami's nose
to make her smile.

At the clinic
crane chisme
fills the waiting room
like a band of pots and pans
until we roll into the clean quiet
of the checkup room.

You and the baby are both doing great!
Twenty weeks and you're right on schedule,
Nurse Sandra says as she show us
the ultrasound of our egg.

It's kicking its little legs, sucking its
little thumb, and turning
away from us like I do
when I'm in bed
and I don't want
to wake up.

Mami pays one hundred dollars for the visit
because we don't have that insurance
we'd have if we weren't cranes.

Estoy feliz, she says, *the baby is okay.*

Mami and I almost bounce back out
into the cold sun of the morning
that pours itself
onto my East LA
like liquid gold
the color of corn.

A SECRET FOR AN ANGEL

St. Rose of Lima is super crowded.
It's La Virgen de Guadalupe's day.
But we wiggle our way
up to the big statue of
La Virgen, who has
more flowers than
a garden.

I give her angel
a secret crane poem.
   My wish for dulzura for Papi.

I fold it into
a tight origami triangle
and cram it between the angel's
hairy head and the crescent.

It's almost a secret because
you can see a big chunk of my
name and date on the triangle fold.
  ita–December 12

66

FRIENDSHIP PARK

I need to see mis amores,
Papi says when he calls.
The achy feeling
of wanting to be with him
          splits   my heart   just a little more open.
Mami's eyes flood with tears
when she says,
And we need to see you, cariño.

A crane told me
there is a way for us to meet
at a place called Friendship Park
at the Tijuana / San Diego border.
Though, we would be divided
by a fence.
          Really, Papi?
          Maybe we can at least hold your hand?
          Maybe you can touch Mami's nest!
          Maybe we can hug you!
I don't know for sure
but wouldn't that be sweet, Plumita?
          I wish we could do that.
          Wait, could we?
Well, I could take a Friday-night bus
to Tijuana and be there by Saturday
when the park is supposed to open.

Mami jumps in up.
I could ask your brother, Juan, to drive us there?

Is Tijuana far, Papi?
Not as far for you as it is for me.
Please, Papi!
Please, Mami!
Could we try?
We could! Why not, mi'ja?

Papi, do you think it would be safe?
I ask, suddenly remembering
how ICE took him.
Not at Friendship Park, they say
that place is made for meeting!

My wings begin to wiggle when he says,
*Let's talk to Tío Juan
and see what he says.*

BORDER BEACH

Tío Juan plays Norteñas
nonstop in the car
as we drive to meet
Papi in San Diego.
      Tío Juan's, Tía Raquel's,
         Tina's, and Mami's heads
    bounce to accordions and horns.
        My jittery mind does jumping jacks.

Mami brought Papi homemade gorditas
filled with picadillo and her too-spicy-for-me salsa.
I brought him a new crane poem
and his pillowcase
    so he can put it in his shirt
    while we visit
    and give his feathered scent
    back to me.

The freeway is crowded with cars
and too many trucks traveling
big and wide and blocking the views
of all I've never seen
    outside of East LA . . .
        Cities, green grassy hills, open skies
    with hawks flying
        and swooping down
    landing on the telephone wires
that look like a necklace
lining the road.

Tina's got the GPS
fixed on Friendship Park
though the signal goes
        in and out.

        Are we close yet?
I ask Tío Juan and Tina every few minutes
and he sighs real deep
but then he gives me a job.
Tell us a story, Betita.

From the back seat where I sit
                squished between
        Tina and Mami
I tell him about how Amparo
and I play Chichimeca warriors
because of the stories Papi once told us.
        Papi said the bravest fighters
                pushed the Spanish away for centuries.
        They would not be conquered.
Just then Mami gets a call from Papi, she says,
He arrived! He said Friendship Park is near a beach!

I can see him now
behind the fence
his bright face
with his broken wings
standing where
the earth meets the ocean
                waiting to hold our hands.

FAITH EXIT

My GPS is jammed, Tina says
looking down at her phone
while more stories pour out of me,
>There are places with huge pyramids
>across the Americas
>where our people
>followed the paths of stars.
>A hundred times bigger than these trucks.

I point to the big rigs we are sandwiched between.

Pa, I think we've gone too far, Tina shouts over me.
>*I'll get off on the next exit.* He moves right,

but a truck's in the way and he can't
so he tries to go around it.

Just as we pass, I read aloud a sign that says,
>"Last US Exit."

Tío Juan's neck twists like an owl's
>to see the road behind him.

¡Hijole! We missed the exit!
>*¿Qué? We did what? Can we make a U-turn?*

We all fling questions at him like rubber band shots.
Ay dios, I'm afraid we have no choice but to go through.

He shakes his head and grips the steering wheel
like we are about to head
>off a cliff.

But we don't.
The car slows with traffic
and we cross what looks
like a gigantic gas station
with an oversized sign that reads,
M E X I C O.

Tío Juan's words run a marathon.
I've got to get back in line. I've got to tell
them it was a mistake. It will be okay. We'll
be okay. We've got our papers. You've got
Fernanda's, right?
Mami nods quickly and holds the bump of her belly.
        Are we okay, Mami? What about Papi? I ask.
She reaches for me and says,
Everything will be alright, Betita.
Be patient. La Virgencita is with us.

She takes my hand and wraps
a string of rosary beads around it.
We have to have faith
that everything will be alright.

MOUTH PATROL

We join the lines of slow-moving cars.
      It's like rush hour in LA! I blurt.
      Is that the US border ahead now, Mami?
Ya, Betita! Tía Raquel shouts. *You're making me nervous.*
Tina pokes me with an elbow.
Mami hushes me by tapping her finger on my lips.
I'm not sure what I said wrong
but I turn off the faucet of my mouth.

As we approach a guard station
the quiet grows in our car.
A man in uniform with the words
"CBP Border Patrol" on his vest
looks in and demands, *Passports, please.*
I'm so relieved it isn't ICE.
Mami hands him the paperwork
Fernanda gave us, and Tío Juan
gives him his and Tina's passports
but he has nothing for Tía Raquel.
The agent looks them over and motions for us
to go park off to the side for inspection.

We get out and Tío Juan's mouth is running again
talking up two more agents who've come
to look through the car and our papers.
I can't make out all they say but I know
Mami's hand
trembles hard
in mine.

CHICHIMECA WARRIORS

Tío Juan's face grows
red as he argues
helicopter arms
moving in every direction.

Suddenly one of the agents
takes Tía Raquel by the arm
and walks her over to an SUV.

Tía Raquel begins to cry
turns back
to scream at Tío Juan and Tina,
Please don't let them take me. Please!

Before I know it, an agent has Mami
by the arm too, but Mami shakes free.
> *¡Espera! Wait, no, no no!*
> *We need asylum, that's what the papers say!*
He grabs her arm again and says coldly,
This isn't enough, you're going in.

I run to hold Mami around the waist
and shout loud at him,
> I am a brave
> Chichimeca warrior!
> You will not take my mami too!
Mami clutches me close.
But my daughter? she begs.
She's going in with you, he cuts.

Tina's and Tío Juan's shock spills
off their faces, their eyes bounce
wild across us.

Tina lifts a quick hand
with her phone to record it.

I swing an angry arm
like a sword
at him.

I repeat louder,
    I am a brave
    Chichimeca warrior!
But the angry-faced agent
slaps my hand away.

                    I spread my wings to fly
              but before I take flight
        they drag us
into the SUV
with Tía Raquel
clipping our wings
when the door
slams
shut.

Mictlan

INSIDE THE SUV

They've tied Mami's and Tia Raquel's
wings behind their backs
with thin plastic strips.

They force-buckle me
to the seat.
      I push
them away, screaming.

I hear Mami's worried voice,
Do what they tell you, Betita!
¡Por favor, amor, por favor!

Mami's and Tia's tears
      collide
with mine as we watch
          Tío Juan and Tina drive away
and others slowly fill the SUV.
Then we finally drive too.
They don't talk to us.
They don't tell us
where we are going.
They don't respond
when Mami pleads
like Fernanda told her
for "political asylum"
because there is
danger waiting for us
in the mountain.

They speak only to tell us,
You have been detained for
breaking United States immigration laws.
You will be processed and
taken to a detention facility.

Detention, like for being
bad at school?
Processed?

Mami prays Tío Juan will
reach Fernanda and that she will
know where to find us
that someone's called Papi
or Amparo's family
to tell them
they've taken us.

Virgencita, protect us, por favor, Mami says.

Though we are
strapped down
I touch Mami's crying face
with one hand.
With the other
I hold our egg
resting in her nest.

I am afraid
it might crack.

THEY DRIVE US THROUGH

a desert to the
"detention facility,"
not cranes, criminals.

A BUILDING MADE OF ICE

When we arrive, a big frozen
concrete monster
            swallows us up
through its heavy mouth.
Doors made of painted iron.

We walk slowly into rooms
one after the other, as cold as stones.
I've heard about this place,
la hielera, an icebox we've seen on the news
that holds cranes in a chill, trying to find home.

We line up with other mothers
and children cranes here too.
Being "processed" like us.
Tía Raquel is taken
to another line with no children.
Could it be because Tina is not with her?

I hold on to Mami's belt loop
as we walk into a room
where they finally release the plastic ties
around her almost-bleeding wrists.
Instead of reaching to rub them
she reaches to fold me
into her warm arms.
She doesn't let go.
Then, her ojos, wet from crying
look to me as if to say,

Be brave, mamita, be brave.

They make her empty her pockets
though all of her things
are in her purse
which they already have.
She holds her breath when
they take the medalla
of La Virgen from around her neck.

She helps me empty my pockets
and what I have, I don't want
to give to them either.
> Fifty cents for chocolate milk
> a shiny concrete rock that glimmers in the sun
> a dried dead bee I collected in the yarda
> and a folded crane poem
> I made just for Papi.

It shows flying Chichimeca warriors
gliding above my school
and reads:
> Warriors swarm
> like bees above us.
> They keep us safe
> while you are away, Papi.
> Betita–February 4

I don't show them Papi's pillow square
stolen away and warming my chest
for no one but me and maybe Mami
to ever smell.

SILVER CAPES

We walk into the ice monster's maze
of chain-link skirts
cages filled with cranes
more shades of tan and brown
than I've ever seen.
Families captured
                    sad faced
                                        worried faced
                                                            crying faced
                                distant faced
                                                            some lying down
                        some standing, arms crossed
                                        others   sitting
no longer wearing wings
            but silver capes
                        that crinkle crackle
            each time they move
or pull the capes closer to their bodies.
            Coughs
                        babies crying
                                    people speaking
            quietly
all a stir in my ears.
            The capes
shuffling and sounding
            so loud inside and outside
                        their murmurs.

Is this where we are headed
when Mami and me are handed
a folded cape each?

Some of them see us   and I can tell
they feel sorry for us. Some stare
                    away from us, maybe wondering
when they will be free.
                    Others close their eyes
                    and clench their fists
        like I sometimes do
when wishing for a nightmare
        to be over.

IT MUST BE ALMOST MY BEDTIME WHEN

we're locked into a
chain-link cage made for cranes
with our silver capes.

HUNGER

My panza grumbles
like trash can opossums
growling in the dark.

I've been too scared to notice
until now.

When I tell Mami,
      Tengo hambre.
She looks down
into me,
Sí, mi amorcito, I am too.

That's when I remember
growing a baby makes
Mami caterpillar hungry
and if she forgets to eat
protein, she gets
woozy headaches
and throw-up sick.

OUR PLACE IN A CAGE

In a cage with what looks
like thirty mothers and children
Mami and I find
a little spot on the concrete floor
enough for one to sit.
Mami goes down first, then
pulls my hand
          pats the space in front of her
for me to sit between
her legs.

She covers us three
with the silver sheets.

The others
watch us, closely
waiting for *us*
while we wait
patiently
for *them* to say
hello.

RIGHT NEXT TO US

Mami searches the stare of a woman
        opposite us.
We are eager for a smile
        but that woman is empty of sonrisas
so Mami looks
to the next
and the next
everyone either too blue or sleepy
to find a way to make pursed lips
turn up
let a sun ray free.

Slowly cranes begin to lie down
pull their foil blankets over the
        ghosts of wings,
        arms, legs,
        their children's too.
The cold is too prickly to sleep.

Mami keeps searching for light
starts to receive shy nods instead
until finally a woman right next to us
with three children of her own
lets an *hola*
bloom in her mouth.

THINK OF DULZURA

To imagine Papi's frown
when he found out

we weren't coming, but taken away
makes me dizzy with sadness.

I want to think of dulzura
like Papi always says

so I imagine we are
in a backyard ballroom fiesta

red, yellow, orange, and green
ribbons shoot through the air

weave themselves into the cages
wrapping us warm with waltzing smiles.

I think of happy Tina
and my one-day quinceañera

I think of spelling a spell
and Virgencita angels with wings

but the cold breeze
stops me.

I squint it away
and dream of ribbons, again

but the chill that rips
up my chicken skin

reminds me, stronger
that we are sitting

in a crowded cell
my little dulzura, dying.

LIGHTS OUT

She says her name is Josefina Ramírez
from a fishing town in El Salvador.
We missed dinner.
It's a miserable tray of frozen vomit-like food.
Tomorrow you will taste it for yourselves.
She fusses with her baby
a round-faced brown crane chick
who scuttles and coughs into her side.

Is this how *I* should keep warm?

She says,
Pronto, the lights
will be out for the night.
But the flashlights will be in our
faces every hour. I'm not sure
what they are checking for.
One thing for sure
they never make it warm here.

Her chicks are
   quiet when
they aren't coughing.
Their faces are bright with rashes.
   Their eyes blink like flickers
   while they scratch their heads.
   Their lips are purple blue with cold.

I pretend I am
        a newborn chick too
and find the warmest
        place to be beside Mami
and the egg.

The crinkle crackle of the blankets
        slowly comes   to a hush after a while
and I feel Mami crying like others
but the
        cough
        cough
        cough of
Josefina's chicks keep punching
                        the night
                until that too
becomes a pounding
        that stones me
to sleep.

BETWEEN SLEEP

I dream of Papi
        flying
            alongside me.

His bright black ojos glisten.

I see his wavy hair
        pushed back by wind.
    Mami is flying too
    the egg under her.
The park and freeways
    below, cars
    like ants
    we are so high.

All of us, soaring.

Then I see him fall
    sudden
with the sound like a
    firecracker
so loud it leaves a ringing
    in my ears.

Then I fall too
though I flap
    my arms
    in a fever.

Mami falls
behind us.

      I scream.

A wet red dot
grows in my chest
which I touch
with my fingers.

I sense we've
      been shot.
By men in the mountain
      below
I can't see?

My heart is a speed train
inside my body
that bursts me awake.

Then, I see the safety pin
      that holds Papi's pillow square
is poking me and
      draws blood.

I'm lying next to Mami
      on the concrete floor.
My panza mumble grumbles
      and my throat
feels like there's
      a big ol' grapefruit

stuck behind my
        tongue.

The lights come on
        inside this cage
and a mass of silver
        foil blankets
begins to stir
        in the ever cold
of this hielera.

JOSEFINA

This is Yanela, Carlos,
and baby Jakeline,
says the mama crane
who spoke to us last night.
I sit up next to Mami
      shiver as I lean into her
and notice their brown faces
soft, in the glowing white light.
I see the shape of their
broken wings
whose tips they use
to   scratch
      scratch
          scratch
their heads.

Josefina pulls lil' Jakie
next to her and begins
sorting through her hair.
I scratch, feeling all
of a sudden an itch
on my own head too.
Mami combs down my feathers
with her hands while we
listen to Josefina tell us
how they got here.

Things were so hard, bien duras, in El Salvador.
I had a food cart where I sold pupusas I made myself.
The marreros came and asked me to pay rent every month
or else they would hurt my children. I paid the first month
but the next month when I didn't want to pay, they beat
me right in front of baby Jakie and said they knew where
Yanela and Carlos went to school. So I paid again though it
left nothing for our expenses. Then I saw them kill a man
for not paying the rent on his cart. I knew we would be
next. We left that night. We hid in another town with my
aunt. My mother sent us the money to pay the coyote to
bring us to the border to turn ourselves in. But they locked
us up behind these fences. Trapped like animals when all we
wanted was a little help.

As we listen
the baby is now free-falling into
the older girl's arms and giggles
so sweetly, but her sister
doesn't break a smile.
Carlos, the boy, sways side to side
like he's almost dancing
with a scowl at me
folded into
the raisin of
his thumb-sucking
face.

WILTED BUGS

When Mami shares
how we ended up here
she holds me closer.

I try to tell Josefina about cranes
but Mami hushes me.

She whispers
to try not to cry.

Josefina shakes her head
while Mami talks
wrinkles her lips tight
tries to calm Jakie on her
lap again and keeps
dipping into the baby's head.

Then, as if she's caught something
between two nails
she presses until something
tiny, so very tiny, pops.

       What was that?

She half smiles like she
feels sorry for me
because I don't know.

Son piojos.
Lice are little bugs

people sometimes get.
Give it a few days here, mi'ja,
and you'll have them too.

Carlos squints
at me, pulls the thumb he's been
sucking out of his mouth,
and lets out a cackle.

The stinker.

Yanela, the girl,
looks down
the entire time.
She droops sad
like wilted flowers.

OFFERING

I offer a smile to Yanela
to try to grow dulzura
in a girl who could be my age
who could be a friend?

Her expression is
as still as steel.

Josefina sees me
          reaching
into the soil of her daughter
wanting to plant a friendship.
She lifts Yanela's chin
          for a second
but as soon as she lets go
Yanela's head buries
down
          into the ground
like lead again.

THE DEEPEST HURT

Josefina takes a shallow breath
        and wants to smile at us
        but it is chased away
by her own gloomy voice
        as she unravels more
        of her story like yarn.

They took my niños from me
days after we arrived here the first time.
They called it "zero tolerance."

I'll never forget how they cried
as they pulled them away
with so much fear inside their tears
I could do nothing about.

Though I begged, day and night,
to have them back
they kept them from me for two months.

The longest, most painful days of my life.
I didn't know if I would ever see them again.

I don't know where they took them
or what they did to them.
I know one thing.

They were different children
when they finally gave them back.

They deported us to Tijuana the next day.
Now they caught us on our second try
to get to Los Angeles, where my sister
is waiting and has a place for us.
            Qué pena, Josefina, I'm so sorry.
Mami taps the back of her hand gently.

Yanela pulls baby Jakie
onto her lap, circles her arms
around her sister, lightly
lays her forehead
on top of the baby's head
like she wants to hide.
Baby Jakie wiggles her head
back and kisses Yanela on
the bottom of her chin.

I wrap the vines of my arms
around Mami's steady leg
so afraid this hurt
will happen to us   too.

FROZEN FOOD

I hear the unlocking of the gate
turn to see two guards with a cart.

One guard yells,
Burros, time to eat!

> They called us donkeys, Mami,
I say to her in disbelief.

Though I'm starving
I grimace at them
but Mami wipes my face
gently with her hand.

I know she is hungry
by the way
she swallows slowly.

We line up to be served
a cardboard tray
holding a burrito
moldy and half-frozen.

Exactly how it feels
to be inside this prison.

CARDBOARD PLAY

I make a game
all by myself
with the cardboard tray
and the paper napkins
I keep.

I suck on small wads of paper
roll and mush them
into the shape of a bird
moist with my spit.

I pretend the tray
is a boat that sails
        no
a nest.

I lay
the bird down
then stuff beneath
its little tail
a perfect oval egg.

Then I make a doll
whose legs I curl
        beneath the bird
and turn her
face   up
to look for

the bluest blue
in the sky.

I catch Yanela
        looking too
so I mash together
another doll.

When I hold it up
to give to her
        she turns
the other way.

A HISS THAT HIDES

One guard's green-gray eyes are
a snake's slithering in the grass.

He is not feathered.
He is not scared.
He is not caged.

He patrols and moves
his overgrown body through us
over and around us.

Circling.

Watching.

A badge with the name "J. Stevens"
like a dangerous mark
across his vest.
A gun holster like a rattle
shaking with each step.

He calls us burros, again.
Donkeys, but really it means stupid.
A word so hurtful Mami never
ever lets me use it.

Don't whine, burros, we saved you from the desert.

He says it in perfectly
round Spanish
the kind of Spanish
that makes you want to
                trust
because it is the Spanish
of Mami's songs
and Papi's stories.

I can't get past
those beady eyes
and the hiss that hides
in every order
he gives.

OPEN TOILET

Half a concrete wall covers a corner of the cage.
Every now and then I see people go in and out.

A toilet flushes and leaves a bitter smell
tells us someone just went.

Mami tells me, *It is okay to go*.
She's gone twice in the night
'cause the egg pushes down on her bladder.

I don't want everyone
to hear me
or smell me go
so I hold it
both number one and number two
until my panza hurts
and I cry as Mami
pulls me through
the cell to the toilet corner
so embarrassed
I bury my face
in my arm.

THE TRASH NEAR

the toilet is piled high and
                overflowing
with wads of toilet paper
from everyone's wipes.

The stink stings my nose.

Mami moves to push
the paper pile down
                into the can
                with her foot
then wraps some paper
around her hands
and picks up
the other toilet paper wads
on the floor.

                I'll help you, I say
covering one hand
and with the other
plugging my nose
with the tips
of my fingers.

I notice some of the stains
peeking through
are red.

What's that, Mami?
That's blood from women
and girls on their regla.

I remember about
the cycles Mami told me
will one day
come to me too.

Pobres, looks like they are
using toilet paper for their necesidades.

We try to wash our hands
but the sink only drops
big drips of water.

ONE HOUR A DAY IN THE LIGHT

Real rays, sun and sky
speckled by clouds
are a relief from
the freezing cold.

I hold Mami's hand
and whisper
        Mami, let's fly
but she looks
at me with the saddest ojitos.
We can't, Betita, remember
our wings have been clipped.

In the light, I can't believe how huge
the white freezing monster is from outside.
I notice all of the fences
the guards at the edges
their guns ready on their belts
to stop us from leaving?

Let's walk, mi'ja, get as warm as you can.
We walk past a group of kids
rubbing rocks on the ground
like chalk
and I wish to
draw something
write something
something big

an S.O.S.
a picture poem
maybe somebody will see
it and get us
out of here.
Maybe?

But I don't want to leave Mami's side for one second.

Mami sings while we walk
and I join in the smallest voice.
We move fast, so fast
sweat bunches up on our foreheads
until it is time to file back in.

How much longer will we be here, Mami?

Mami's worried *I don't know* looks
like a rain cloud just covered her face.

SOUNDS OF SADNESS

Every day and every night
we make different sounds for sadness
a chorus of cranes
        sighs, whimpers,
        cries, soft,
        muffled, echoing loud.
Wheezing. Can this be sad?

Yes, the way it whistles into
and out of little lungs, a rattling
and is followed by
coughs and hacks
        drowning
        in the
        coldest
        tristeza.

ALMOST SOLAS

New cranes crowd our chain-link cell
and the chain-link cells across from ours.

Some look like teens
but they take care, like mamas,
of other kids.

Mami notices they are here
without mothers or fathers.
        Almost alone.

I overhear guards call them
"practically unaccompanied minors."

I don't know
what that means exactly
other than they are here
        almost solas.
Their wings smaller
more hidden
more injured
than the rest of ours.

I see Mami's schoolteacher heart
bend into kindness for them.

I don't know what she might do.

ALMOST SOLAS IN AZTLÁN

Mami gathers the stories
about the almost solitas in broken
bits and pieces.

They are in charge   of their siblings.
They're looking for   their mothers.
They're running from   their fathers.
They were threatened by   gangs.
They've lost   their   way.
They need to   work to send help   back home.
Home in
Guatemala,   Honduras,   El Salvador,   and Mexico
                                                like us.

They are cranes whose
song-like names I try
to catch in my brain . . .
Roxanne,   Mariee,   Allison,   Claudia,   Johanna.

They don't trust us
so, I tell them about the prophecy
in my best Papi Spanish.

The Mexica people came
from Aztlán—the place of the cranes
which we think was an island
on a misty lake, here in El Norte.
Seven tribes
including the Mexica

traveled south like cranes
when Huitzilopochtli—

Who?

The god of war
announced his
prophecy that they
would move south
to build their great
civilization in the
ombligo of the world.

¿De veras? How can this be true?

Because my papi told me so.
He said Aztlán is
our ancestral homeland
and all migrants have come
back home.

But they turn away
like they don't believe
a little kid they just met
like me.

WHAT APPEARS AND FADES

Inside those long, cold days
I wonder what our flock
is doing—Tío Juan, Tina, Diana, Amparo.

I see them looking through
our box of treasures.
Diana, holding our pictures
in her soft hands.

Then, Amparo
playing alone
in our yarda
with a stick
I left behind.

And Tina, missing her mami
and posting a quinceañera makeup
tutorial on her Gram page
and getting so many likes.

When I try to imagine
Papi, his face fades

           into fog.

YELLOW HAIR SHOWER

Mami says it's been a week since
we were swallowed by
this monster.
        A week?
It feels as long as a year.

We line up for showers
though we don't have
anything else to wear.
Some cranes are covered
in dirt so thick it's hard to tell
the real color of their clothes.

But then they give us
a dingy towel and
a bag of old clothes
for us to fish for anything clean.
We find
        T-shirts
        sweatshirts
        the biggest, boxiest underwear
        and pants.
They want us to throw our
old things into the trash.

I turn to Mami and shake my head.
I don't want to give up my blouse.
I want to keep Papi's pillow square close.

The woman guard with yellow hair
stands above me.
She is a tower when I look up.
Her hand on her hips, she
clears her throat and
fumes,

Now!

I stomp my feet on her foot
accidentally when I sass back,

No!
I don't want you to take my blouse!

Mami pleads with me,
Betita, por favor. Don't make trouble.

The guard grabs me by the arm
shakes my body like a sheet
and starts to pull up my blouse.

Mami steps in like wind.
No la toques, you will not touch my little girl!
I touch who I want!
You will not!

Mami snatches me away
with mama-bear strength.
The guard goes to hit Mami,
but the guard only
scratches her arm.

Mami pulls me behind her
and looks at Yellow Hair
           right in the snake of her eyes.

Do as you are told, wetback!

Mami doesn't answer, but
she also doesn't move.

Behind her, I quickly pull my hand
into my blouse and remove
the pin that holds my pillow square
and sneak them into the new clothes
that have dropped to the floor.

When I come up, I pull off my blouse
hold it against my bare chest
and stare brick hard up at Yellow Hair
until she begins to move on and says,
That's more like it.

SICK

All the women and girls have to bathe
in one big open shower.

I want to fly away.

I can tell Mami is crying
though she turns me away
so she can wash my hair.
I hear the little gasps
of breath she takes laced
with the tiniest squeak.

I have to close my eyes
but I open my mouth
to swallow the shower water because
inside our cell there is no fountain
and the handwashing sink is broken
so we drink from the toilet tank.
I pretend it is raining
and Amparo and I
are in our yarda
tongues out
collecting the drops . . .

Then, suddenly, I hear Mami gag.
I turn to see her folded over
holding her nest
and throwing up
a liquid mess

all over the shower.
Ay, Virgencita, she cries.

Yellow Hair comes
in with her baton out
grabs Mami
by the hair and pulls
up her head
growling, *What now, wetback?*
But Mami continues
to throw up
so Yellow Hair lets her go
and laughs at her.

When Mami is done
I am her cane.
I help her rinse off
and walk her to
the changing area.

I look back to see
Josefina running the water
over the mess Mami made.

Are you okay, Mami? I ask
the worry and the smell making
me want to throw up too.

I need to lie down, mi'ja.
I just need to lie down.

THE SHAPE OF A NEST

My lap makes a pillow
for Mami's head while
she lies on the frozen concrete floor.
I tucked her in snuggly
with both of our silver blankets.

I stroke her head quietly
searching for dulzura.
Rub the pillow square against her cheek.
I wish I knew the words to the song
about a paraíso so I could sing it to her.
Instead, I hum it.

I stare at her brown crane-skin
paler than before
and her thick, wavy hair
still wet and so deep brown
it shines like ocean stone.

I follow the shape of her body
the way her nest makes
her back bend into an
      S
and her front into an
      O.

Two months until it hatches.

I want to ask Mami if she
thinks we will be out of here
by then, but she is sleeping now.

Right before I close my eyes
              I see the O of her nest
              turn into a Q.
        I know our baby chick is moving
and suddenly
everything feels better.

I WAS AN EGG ONCE

Before we flew across the deserts

before we landed in East LA

before Tío Pedro went missing

before we found our flock here

before I knew of picture poems

before we were trapped in a monster

I was an egg inside of Mami

inside Mexico, stirred, cooked, and hatched

right from the nesting hearts

of a singing Mami and a dreaming Papi

whose mountain home was filled with love.

FAKE FEEL BETTER

Is there a doctor I can see?
Mami asks Josefina.
She answers first
with a big sigh, then says,
You have to get better on your own
or you have to fake it. They can take
your girl from you, if you aren't well.
Yanela turns out her lower lip
scrunches it against her top in agreement.

I hear this and it scares a chill all over me.

> Mamita, will you please get better fast?
> I don't want to be away from you.
> Please.
> Please.
> Please!

Mami struggles to lift herself.
Baby Jakie claps happy hands
together to see her get up.

Mami presses my cheeks together
her always cariñito
and says, *Sí, mi amorcito. I will.*

Though the panic keeps
running
wild
all over my head.

MAYBE

I lean against the chain-link
and watch Mami lie back down to sleep.

I think Tío Juan
maybe never called Fernanda?

Maybe he was too scared to call?
Maybe he and Papi are looking for us?

Maybe Fernanda abandoned us too
and we will never leave this dangerous place?

Maybe there is no such thing
as finding dulzura in our struggle?

Maybe we will never see Papi again?

Maybe I will forget the flower of his face?

AN ITCH SO BAD

The next morning
I'm up before everyone.
My head itches
so badly all I want to do is
S C R A T C H
S C R A T C H
S C R A T C H!

Oh oh! ¿Piojos?

Mami is still sleeping
and I'm not waking her
to worry her more.

So I just do it.

I use my fingernails to dig
into the itchy craziness in my hair
and it makes me
feel so   much better for
a tiny second
before I've got to do it
again
and again.

I see Yanela catch me
scratching, so I put
my hand down quickly.

Her eyes aren't floating into space.

She smiles shyly at me
then gently waves me over
to sit next to her.

Maybe she wants to check
to see if what I fear
I have is for real.

I'm so glad Carlos is snoring away.

BEDHEAD LICE

Yanela is a quiet mouse
but moves her fingers
through my bedhead
parting and p u l l i n g
parting and p u l l i n g
what feels like one
long strand at a time.

I ask her,
          Do you think I have piojos?
And she is silent.

          How do you know it isn't the soap
          left over from the shower?
And she is silent.

          Do you speak English?
And she is silent.
But when I ask the same in Spanish
she finally answers to say,
No.

I have to rearrange my mind.
My question seems stupid.
I should have known.
Everyone in here speaks Spanish, mostly.
Mami and I are the few who speak both.

Then, Yanela quickly chases
        and catches
        and crushes
a critter between her fingers
with the same tiny pop
her mom made before.

        Are you ever going to say anything, Yanela?
I use my East LA Spanish.
        And still she is silent.

I figure, I will talk to *her* instead.
I begin to tell her
all about who we are.

        We once lived like cranes
        in a place called Aztlán
        where we were free to roam
        across the land . . .

I can tell she is listening
because she   pauses
but when I turn my head
she goes back to parting and p u l l i n g.

She works on my head quietly
and I keep going on and on
spinning and tangling up
all of Papi's stories
until I notice Mami start
to stir awake.

I dash over and lie next to her
and I look at her slightly puffy
eyes still bloodshot from yesterday.

I want my face to be the one
to make her well.

I BLAME THE CLAWS

I feel better this morning.
It all caught up to me,
Mami explains.

I don't blame her.
The food has been so gray
and what that yellow-haired guard
did to us made me so scared
I got lice.
Well, maybe I got it without her
          but still.

I check Mami's arm to see
          three
          red
          streaks
that Yellow Hair's awful claws
left on her skin.

Mami thinks that Yellow Hair
descends from cranes, like us
because her hair is bleached yellow
and her last name is Pacheco.
          But she called us wetbacks, Mami?
Then, I scratch my head, wildly.
Mami sighs so deeply
just closes her eyes
and nods.

ALL ABOUT CRANES

After the breakfast Mami and I refuse to eat
Yanela signals me over to her
with a tiny wiggle of her pointer finger.

Tell me again about the cranes,
los tocuilcoyotl, she whispers
as she turns my shoulders
away from her and picks apart my hair.

       There once was a great migration
       brown-and-white cranes
       swept their way south.
       They flew to find the great city
       in the belly button of the universe
       which was a tiny island where they saw
       the most amazing thing—an eagle
       devouring a serpent on top of a cactus.
       So they built their city around the tiny sacred island
       and filled in the shallow water with earth.
       There they would dance, and croon rattle their songs,
       and farm, and build nests, and make magic.
       And one day, the migration was reversed
       and the magical cranes flew north
       back to the place where they began
       to dance, croon rattle their songs, farm,
       build nests, and be magical there once again.

If our wings weren't clipped, Yanela,
we could fly too.

I look over my shoulder to see
Yanela's itsy-witsy smile.

PIOJO INITIATION

When Yanela is done,
she folds my hair into two
pretty, long French braids.
But then I feel a really hard YANK!
I'm shocked
and I turn around
feeling so betrayed.
        Ow!
I see Carlos laughing out loud
with his wet thumb outside his mouth.

Yanela whacks him on the arm.

Hey! I'm just welcoming her
to the piojo club. It's her initiation!

All I dare do is scrunch my nose at him
while I stick out my tongue.

I've just made a friend
who I don't want to lose
but I could do without
        her little booger of a brother.

MAMI GATHERS A NEW FLOCK

I start counting the days
        two weeks now
    locked in here
    with one hour of light
        the coughing sounds of sadness
    Yellow Hair and Snake Eyes
    surrounding us every minute
        no Papi
        no Tía Raquel
        no school
        no doctor
        no Fernanda
        no Virgencita
        no way to make a picture poem
        and no way to send it.

Mami and I
have learned
how each crane
in our cage
    was trapped here
and they know
about us, Tía Raquel,
and Papi too.

Mami has made friends
with the almost
    solitas
some who have cried
in her arms

after a little more
conversation.

Some are
just eighteen
and scared
to be treated
          like adults.
They don't know
how to be parents
all of a sudden.

At night
they quietly gather
to sleep near Mami.
I think they feel
like me,
          safer
when she is around.

VOLAMOS

Yanela and I push
through the gate
when it is outdoor time.

We chase each other
inside this barbwire desert.
I yell as I run beside her,

>   Open your arms like this, Yanela!
>   Can you feel the wind tickling?
>   Can you feel your plumas?

Her laugh is as big as the sun.

>   We are cranes, Yanela, somos tocuilcoyotl!
>   We are flying home!

We run and run
eyes sometimes closed
our feet   just   barely
touching the ground.

TWISTING TOOTH SHOE

Today while outside
Carlos is twisting on
the pavement next to Josefina,
who rubs, rubs, rubs
his arm and back
while he wails
and wails.

Yanela tells us
he has a toothache
when we approach
to see if we can help.
He sees me and growls
plus, throws his shoe at me!

Josefina says,
Perdón, es que he's in a lot of pain.

As I back up from him
he starts sucking his mouth
into a tight little knot
grimacing and making
the angriest grunt
until it reaches a high pitch.
Then, suddenly, he opens
his ojos wide
            and spits up blood.

Josefina swoops up Carlos
into her arms, looks at Mami
then at baby Jakie and Yanela.
Mami understands and says,
Sí, Josefina, descuida, run!

Yanela runs after her mother
and baby Jakie starts to cry loudly
though Mami is now holding her.

From the other end of the yard
we can see Josefina yelling for help
Yanela standing next to her, pleading too.

The guards open the gate and
only let Josefina and Carlos
through, leaving Yanela
clinging and trying to climb
the chain-link fence
crying, *Mamá, don't leave me!*
Mamá, don't leave me again!

I run over to be with her
but when I get there
she's as broken
      as glass
her heart
      so shattered
and
      splintered

I can't
     pick up
          the pieces.

UNBELIEVABLE TO SLEEP

Inside the cell
minutes stretch
into hours since
we last saw
Josefina and Carlos.

Mami gathers all three of us
into her warm mama body
made of soft feathers.
There is much more
of her to share now.

She calms their cries
takes turns stroking our hair.
Everything will be all right.
A dentist is seeing your brother
and they will help him.
Your mami is making sure of it.
She will be back before you know it.

She convinces me
but by the look
of the hard quiet
of the sisters
I don't think
they believe Mami.

Yanela stares
over and beyond us
so absent, so far.

But then, Mami starts to sing
the song about a paraíso
and the chick in the egg
          starts to kick
which we feel on our faces
as we snuggle against her.

And this way
around Mami
we are all lulled
and pulled
into her song
and we sleep.

AT THE ROOT

When we wake up
        Josefina is asleep
with all of her children
        scattered
around her.

I whisper Mami awake,
        What happened, Mami?
Mami answers with closed lids.
They took him to a dentist
outside the detention center.
He's all right now.
He had to have a root canal.

I never want to have a root canal
and have to throw a shoe at someone
because of the pain,
I think to myself.

THROAT SCHOOL

Later that day
Mami makes an announcement
to everyone in our cell.

She is going to start
an escuelita.
            A school? Why, Mami?
What else could children do here but learn?

But we don't have any materials,
says one of the girls named Griselda.

I promise, you will not need
anything but this up here,
            she says while tapping
            her finger on her temple,
and this right here,
            and tapping her throat.

Mami's made enough friends
that no one says no.

TOILET PAPER SONGS

Dos y dos son cuatro
cuatro y dos son seis
seis y dos son ocho
y ocho dieciséis.

Mami sings sweetly and we repeat
laughing and tripping over tongue twisters too.

Rápido corren los carros
cargados de azúcar al ferrocarril.

Her songs make the time
and the cold disappear
for a couple of hours a day.

My voice grows raspy
so Mami tells me
to turn my volume down or hum.

While we sing, Yanela and I make
more moist toilet paper sculptures
            birds, turtles, bunnies, bears,
            and Belle in her dress
to add to our collection
resting on cardboard trays
stained with food.

TO THE OFFICES

When we finish
singing our seven times tables
to the tune of "Happy Birthday"
the guard calls Mami over.

We all hold still.
Maybe she's in trouble
for changing our cries to songs?

Mami turns back to me
to say there is a phone call waiting
but I can't come with her.
She brings her thumb
and pointer finger together
but leaves a small space
between
which is Mexican for
      wait, just a little.

I wonder who it is
as I stare at Mami wobbling
out of the gate and
through the maze
of fencing to the offices.

I sit near Yanela's family
suddenly feeling
alone.

THE CALLER

My heart jumps inside
my ribs when I see Mami
return, finally!

She is shaking her head
slowly, her face
a prune of worry.

      Was it Papi?
      What did he say?
No, Betita. It was the attorney, Fernanda.
      When will she get us out of here, Mami?
      I want to go home.
      Back to our house in East LA.
We can't go back, corazón
our house has been emptied.
Diana had to pack it up
because our rent was due.
She sold the furniture
but saved our important things
pictures and memories, your favorite teddy.
They're with Tina and Tío Juan now.
      Did they keep my crane poems?
I don't know, mi'ja.
Mami brushes my eyelashes
to try to wipe away my almost crying.

Fernanda said she was sorry
it took her a month to find us.
She called every detention facility
but because we were moved
from Tijuana where we were taken in
it was really difficult.

What is she going to do?
She is going forward with our case for political asylum.
But it will be a while before we get a court date.
And we will have to stay here until that time.
But then, she isn't sure if they will grant us permission.
We might be deported like many of our friends here fear.

What about Papi?
Does he know where we are?
Not yet because she only found us today.
But she's spoken to him and told him
she was doing her best to find us.

Mami, I whisper, did you tell her
they hurt us here?
I couldn't, Betita, they were listening.
But she will be coming to see us in a couple of days
and she's bringing you some crayons and paper.
She wants you to draw your picture poems again
because she'll need them as testimony.

As what?
Your own story of what has happened.

My wings tingle
for the first time
since we got here
like they used to
when I was about
to fly into the sky.

CROWBAR BLUE

If I could draw a crane poem now
      I would paint us blue
            shivering in this cell
                and Fernanda with a crowbar
                      knocking down guards
                            breaking open the lock
                                that keeps us trapped.

I would write:
        Super Fernanda comes
            to try
            to pry
            us all out.
            Betita—some day in March

ARMPIT BAND

I teach Yanela how to make
farting noises with her armpits
like Amparo taught me.

Prrrrprtoot! Prrrrprtoot!

Carlos catches on when we practice
but its baby Jakie who cracks up first
so we keep going
        like a band of musicians
        trying to make music.
The more we armpit fart
the more the baby laughs
and soon
her little contagious chuckles
        make everyone release
            a smile and then
                little laughs and
                out-loud laughter
                of their own
            that spreads like a
                  wildfire
            of uncontrollable joy
        from every
crane in the cages!

Our laughter is an applause
the guards can't
do anything
to stop.

THE DREAMER

A shock of loud curse words
rips through the building
in rippling punches
later that day.
        We all look to see
two guards pushing
        an angry   young woman   forward
her hands tied behind her back.
        Her hair is wagging
           like wild, windblown grass.

Don't push me, you piece of scum!
I know my rights!
You're filth! You hear me,
you get paid to be filth for the government!

But then they
        push   her   harder!
So   hard
she falls
to her
knees.

Shut up, perra! Say hello to the icebox!

But this makes her angrier, and she
screams her anger into the air
like a warrior about to charge.

You're the animals, look at you!
Malditos sean, heartless animals!

They get her up and open the
gate to our cell, and give her a shove.
When they cut the plastic ties loose
she lunges at one of the guards.

The guard's fist smashes into her nose
which sends her back like a rag doll.
Then the other guard rushes her
while she is down
         and kicks
               and kicks
         and kicks
her in the stomach
              and in the face
       until she is   still
crying
and
breathing
a heavy
and steady
pain.

Anáhuac

GROUNDED

She's a broken crane
with wounded scattered feathers
the guards leave behind.

MARISEL

She wipes her bloody nose with her
gray T-shirt that says "#AbolishICE!"
and then bangs the concrete floor
with her open hand.
¡Malditos!

She is a heated tornado.

The fear freezes me
but I watch Mami get close.

Take your time, chiquita, Mami says softly,
helps her sit up, and then
hands her a wad of toilet paper from her pocket.
The girl stares at Mami for a second
and then down to her big belly
and somehow, the girl's heat fades
with a big breath.

¿Cómo te llamas?
          Marisel.
*I'm Gabriela and that girl
over there is Betita, my daughter.*
Marisel looks at me
blinking tearfully
and shrugs one shoulder
as if to say, *Who cares?*

I want to make sure you are okay, is all.
          Gra-gra—, Marisel stutters to say it at first

but then it comes out slowly,
> *Gracias.*
> *Once the bleeding stops*
> *I think I'll be okay.*
Mami then comes to get her silver blanket
and takes it to her.
You can cover yourself with this.
Marisel looks up at Mami
and says it again,
> *Thank you.*

As Mami walks back to me
a guard bangs his baton
on the chain-link fence
and glares at Mami with
an *I'm watching you* scowl.

WHY, MAMI?

       Why did you do that, Mami?
I cross my arms at her
annoyed.
The rest of the cell is statue still
stunned by what just happened.

Mami raises her calm eyebrows at me.
I do what I can for those who need help.
I would do it for you.
       But you don't even know her.

Beeetiiitaaa, she says, dragging the vowels in my name
while undoing the knot of my arms,
since when did we stop doing
what our hearts tell us is right?
       What if the guards had come back for you?
But they didn't and that girl
really needed someone's help.
She holds my floppy wrists
with her caring hands and nods
like she hopes I will agree.

I hug Mami and smoosh my head
on the top of the nest
feeling so selfish
and wrong
for forgetting
what a flock
does for one another.

THAT NIGHT

I try to sleep between
        Mami and Yanela.
Maybe it is the lightless air
or Mami's sleeping breaths
or what she said
about our hearts
but I get the nerve up to
ask Yanela what happened
when they took her
away from her mother.

You don't want to know.
        I do!
It's too terrible to tell.
        I still want to know.
        If you want to tell it.

Yanela stares at the ceiling
taps her fingers on her chest lightly.
She begins to speak softly.

I'll tell you because
you are my friend now, Betita.
'Cause we're cranes.
Promise never to say a word
to another living soul? ¿Ninguna?
        I promise. Changuitos que sí.
I cross two fingers in a swear above her.
She wiggles to the side to whisper near my ear,

We were taken to a place that looked
like a hospital but wasn't with lots of other kids.
Babies too. There was not one of us
who didn't cry and cry for our parents at first.
I tried to keep at least Jakie with me because
she was a girl but they wouldn't let me.
She went with the babies. I stayed with the older girls.
Carlos with the boys. They screamed at us
to do this and that, rules, like here. They gave us shots.
Right on the arm! Lots of them, though we'd already
got them in El Salvador. They made my arm swell up
like a balloon and gave me a fever. But that wasn't the worst.

      Did they hit you?
Not me but sometimes they hit the kids
who tried to run out the doors or cried too loudly.
They would scream, "Shut up, shut up!"
But that wasn't the worst.

      Really?
Then, Yanela pauses for such a long
time I think she's fallen asleep.
There was a man who cooked our food
who would lock me in the closet with him.
He did things.
He told me it was supposed to feel good
but it didn't. It hurt me so so bad, I threw up.

      In the closet?
Uh-huh. All over him. Then he stopped.
So I started making myself sick
each time he trapped me.

      Did you tell the people there?
He said if I told anyone, he would make it
so that I never saw my mama again.

So I didn't tell the grown-ups
but I told all of the kids to run
when he came near them.
           Pobrecita,
I begin to say, but the sadness I feel
for her gets all tangled inside my
voice box with the biggest tears.
           I'm   so   o   soorry Yan   ela.
Shshsh, Betita, you said you wouldn't say anything.
She covers my mouth with her hand.
I pull it away and give it a little squeeze
and nod and let the tears roll down
for Yanela but also to imagine
what would happen if I was
ever taken away from Mami.

That night
there are more coughs
than normal
more cries
more sighs
our fear
a bear
roaring   in the   dark.

THE WILDEST CRANE

I wake to someone talking loudly.
When I look over, I see it is Marisel
and I cover my face with my hand.

I mean, why don't they turn up
the heat in here? Because it is a form
of torture, that's why. Just like my
beat-down, that's a kind of torture too.
And taking away niños from their
parents in here, dang, that's the worst
kind of torture. It's straight jacked up.
You see, they don't want this to be cool
like we are at summer camp or something.
They want it to be as cruel as possible
so that we want to leave the country.

She's speaking in a singsong way
moves her hands and arms
like she's a rapper, and she's
talking to a teen and her sister
who got here a few days ago.

Pero, what they don't want to admit
is that our people have been here
since before there were borders.
We are indigenous to this land
and they, THEY are the illegal immigrants
who came to this continent without
an invitation and colonized.

And here we are, having to wait
in this freezing freaking cage
having to put up with all of their mistreatment
just so that we can get permission
to live in this damn country.

The whole cell is awake now
listening to her say things
I didn't know.
When the teen asks her where she
is from, her talking gets faster.

Technically, Mexico but in reality
I spent most of my life in Southeast LA
and so have my parents and all of my friends.
But like I said, these are the Americas
and I'm indigenous to this place, just like you.

Something about how she is saying
what she is saying pulls me and Yanela over
and we sit to listen to Marisel keep
spinning her words into our ears.

Mira, I'm a Dreamer and I had to do all
sorts of things to get DACA, you know,
Deferred Action for Childhood Arrivals
which was supposed to protect me
but that didn't stop them from putting
me in here. I was at a rally at the border
and made a speech about the abuse
of the immigrant community by ICE.
I locked arms with people

to build a bridge between
Mexico and here, but because
I happened to stand on the Mexican
side of the border they said
I violated my DACA by crossing
and threw me in here.
They're trying to deport me now.
I did nothing but speak out. Dang, if I had
my phone, I'd be posting about this right
now to my 10K followers. It would go viral.

I am trying to understand Marisel.
Her loud singsong raps despite her two growing
black eyes and swollen lip, how is it that
she has more followers than Tina, the things
she knows about our history
that is sort of like Papi but angrier
and she's teaching us like Mami but wilder.

I've never met a crane like her before.

168

DON'T MIND SHARING

The next day doesn't come fast enough.
Fernanda should be here soon.
The hours   lean   against
a   long   breath   of waiting.

We are as eager to see Fernanda
as we are for a drink of pure water
unchlorinated water
not from the shower or toilet tank.

We learn from Marisel
that Fernanda is also hers!
Mami says it is the best
kind of coincidence.

She asks Mami to please
tell Fernanda she is here too
because we figure she doesn't know.

I don't mind helping Marisel
anymore because she reminds me
of a music star, thick with fire.
Everything *really is* "jacked up" in here.

I sway and bop my head
to every one of Marisel's words
sprouting truths
so true   I can feel
my wings regrowing
in real time.

GATEKEEPER

When Fernanda finally comes
Yellow Hair calls Mami
from the gate three times
in a voice that sounds
like screeching tires,

        Gabriela   Quintero,
              Gabriela   Quintero,
                    Gabriela   Quintero.

We scramble to the gate.
Mami holds my hand firmly
as we begin to move, but
Yellow Hair stops me
with her baton.

       Not the kid. I didn't call her.
But we are seeing the same attorney.
       I don't care.
If you don't let me bring her
I will tell my attorney once I see her
and you'll have to let her through anyway.
With a sideways grimace, Yellow Hair lifts
her icy baton and
lets me
pass.

FERNANDA

When we come into
the room where Fernanda
is waiting, she has no crowbar.
There is only a small table
between us and a small stack
of papers and folders.

She wears a bubbly smile that makes
me so happy at first but makes Mami
burst into tears, which then makes *me*
dig my face into Mami's side and cry too.

Fernanda doesn't say anything but
puts her hand on my hand
makes a curvy *so sorry* look.
          I feel like she understands.

After she has given us a moment
to come back to ourselves
she begins to explain
and I try hard to follow.

Entry into the United States without permission
is a misdemeanor. The lowest kind of infraction
in the US. The government in power has created
stricter laws now and is punishing these misdemeanors
with indefinite detention until the cases are resolved.
But, another way to get out is to post a bail bond
of twenty thousand dollars.

Mami's eyes grow wide, fill back up
with tears, which she wipes away
with the back of her hand.
Sí, I understand.
　　　　　But we don't have twenty thousand?
I say, trying not to be whiny.
Fernanda doesn't hesitate,
I know, Betita. Most migrants seeking asylum don't.
The only good news is I have a court date for you
in a month, before the baby is born.
I asked to expedite it due to special circumstances.
We don't want the baby to be born inside detention.
They don't have the necessary personnel
or the right facility for it to be safe.

I hadn't thought of that
and I feel like an hija mala suddenly.
I'd been thinking about Tía Raquel
Mami and me getting out
about seeing Papi again
　　　　　about flying.
I never thought what would happen
to Mami if the egg hatches in here.
Now I'm thinking
what would happen to *me*
if it does hatch?

Have you talked to Beto? Mami asks suddenly.

Yes, he wants to speak to you
but the facility only allows calls from attorneys.
He said he loves you very much and

seeking asylum is the right thing
to do, to please hold on.

A warm sweet heat fills
my head.
I miss Papi so much.

Betita, I brought you a notebook and crayons.
Your mom did such a good job collecting
all of those documents for me, but
we need to collect some from you.
I saw your gallery of drawings hanging
in the kitchen when I visited your house.
I think you'd be able to tell us a little about
what has happened to you, to show the judge.

She hands the guard standing next to her
the crayons and notebook, and he takes them
to inspection off to the side.
        But I made those for Papi.
        Not for a judge.
I can mail them to him in Mexico
once we get a copy.
        Fernanda. What day is it?
It's March fifth. Why do you ask, Betita?
        My picture poems need to know.

Then Mami whispers hard,
It is a nightmare in here, Fernanda.
They treat us worse than animals.
We are sleeping on a concrete floor
twenty or thirty of us to a cage

it is so cold the children are sick
their lips and hands are blue
they have lice and rashes
some hardly want to talk
some children don't even want to play.
They beat a girl here yesterday
who says she is your client too.
Marisel Doming —

      Marisel Dominguez? The Dreamer?
Yes, she was arrested a couple of days ago
and brought here. She asked us to tell you
she is here.

      Is she okay?
She's got two black eyes
and her lip is swollen a bit
but she is still pretty feisty.

      Thank you. I will request to see her next.
      Marisel is one of our most important leaders.

I knew there was something about her.
I just knew it.

Before we leave Fernanda
she tells us she will bring up
the conditions with her colleagues.
Hopefully they'll find a way to sue them
since this is a private prison
not the government's and our complaints
aren't the only ones
but until then, she is sorry.

This is
all
she can do.

AN UNDERSTANDING

After seeing Fernanda
Marisel is hush quiet.

She isn't pointing out how
jacked up everything is
or trying to inhale
everyone's arrival story.
She is looking at us
with extinguished eyes
I've seen before
in Mami.

She must be understanding
for the first time
    how badly her wings
    have been cut.

MY VERY OWN

I curl my hands around
my very own crayons
take a deep breath of their
salty sweet smell
feel a pulsing tingle
to hold my brand-new
two-hundred-page spiral notebook
and fill it with
my very own words.

Though it might be weird
I can't wait to *spell* again.
Yes, spell out my favorites
that tumble and rumble
sulk and hulk
        twirl and swirl
inside my head.

But then, Carlos is lurking.
I can feel he wants to take them.
I squint my eyes at him
while I sit on *my* supplies
I will NOT be sharing.

HASHTAG REVOLUTION!

The next day Marisel
awakes spitting out ways
she is going to get
out of here.

Marisel gave
Fernanda permission
to post for her
on social media.
She is going to get
Marisel's girlfriend,
Erika, involved too.
Marisel says Erika
has 12K followers on
her Gram page alone.
They are starting
a hashtag campaign
to bring attention
to how they are
caging cranes.

I jump in,
        My cousin Tina has a thousand followers too!
But Marisel shrugs her shoulders
and keeps talking.
She tosses out some
ideas for us to hear,
#FreeMarisel
#IAmADreamerDetained

#MigrantsHoldUpTheWorld
#AsylumIsLegal
#StopMigrantDetention
#NoHumanIsIllegal

I offer up
            #FreeTheCranes
but Marisel twists
her eyebrows at me
and swats at the air
in front of her with
her hand, erasing my hashtag.
We need to start
a revolution for us, Betita,
not for some birds!

I guess only
Mami and Yanela
really believe.

UP INSIDE

Too many days have passed to keep count.
A raspy wet cough sits in my lungs
and barks itself up each time
I try to talk.

Mami lies down more now
when she isn't singing
and teaching us.
She is having trouble
keeping any food down
when she does eat.
Sometimes I pick out
the best part of my food
to see if the better parts will help her
keep something in her belly
but nothing helps.

I'm having trouble remembering the sound of Beto's voice,
she says. *Maybe it is my nervios.*

I feel a tearing inside.
         No, Mami, he's here. Right here.
I pull out my papi square
put it to her nose
but now it only smells like
me.

I sit near
my resting mami
and keep scribbling onto paper
how much my heart hurts.

INSIDE MY ALAS:

I've given my notebook a name.
Tagged it right on the
cover—"Alas."

I flip through Alas to see what I've done:

> I drew a picture of Papi as a flying crane.
>> You are the sound of
>> crane trumpets that
>> sing their love into the sky.
>> Betita—March 5

> I drew what the monster looks like from the outside.
>> We've been swallowed
>> by a monster
>> so cold it turns
>> our hopes frozen.
>> Betita—March 7

> I drew a maze of cages and crying cranes.
>> Across from us there is another cage
>> with more cranes and their kids
>> and almost solitas kept from flying.
>> Betita—March 8

> I drew a picture of Papi in his construction hat with tears
> on his cheeks.
>> I know you miss us, Papi, like we miss you.
>> Betita—March 9

I drew a picture of pregnant Mami lying on the floor near the fence.

> Mami and the egg curl into an O
> when she is sick.
> Sometimes the egg's kick
> doesn't make her a Q.
> *Betita—March 10*

I drew the food they expect us to eat.

> They give us black moldy burritos for breakfast
> sometimes nothing for lunch
> and frozen black moldy bread for dinner.
> *Betita—March 11*

I drew Yanela, Carlos, Jakie, and me, jagged like we are vibrating.

> Piojos bounce off our heads.
> The itch drives us CRAZY!
> *Betita—March 12*

I drew a girl trapped in a closet, crying.

> Sometimes big people hurt us
> and we can only cry, tell other kids,
> or throw up.
> *Betita—March 13*

I drew a boy holding his mouth and a shoe.

> A root canal
> makes you
> throw a shoe.
> The dentist is too far away.
> *Betita—March 14*

I drew Marisel after she got beaten.

> When you sing
> the truth
> not even a beating
> will quiet it.
> Betita—March 15

I drew a new family.

> We met a girl today who is scared
> like her mother.
> She is from an island
> where they speak Creole and a little Spanish.
> Her name is Ellie, nine like me.
> Betita—March 16

When Papi gets these
I imagine he will hang them
on a clothesline in a field
of agaves where he works.

WITHOUT HOPE

"Despair" is a word I learned from Marisel today.
We can't despair, she says, after Fernanda tells us
our court date has been pushed back
because there aren't enough judges
for all of the immigration cases.
Plus, their hashtag campaign
hasn't made an impact at all.

Despair is to be without hope, lost.

I feel despair drip into my veins
like a poison starting to take over.

I wonder if
we are cranes at all.

STRIKE!

We have to strike! These conditions
and the waiting are criminal,
Marisel says as she walks back and forth
a few steps at a time.

If we can't have a movement on the outside
we can create it from the inside.
Mami asks, *What kind of strike?*
Marisel stops her pacing to look
seriously at Mami.

A hunger strike.
Some of the mothers in our cell
gasp a little, some shake their heads,
but almost all of them begin to nod
in agreement. So do all of the solitas.

Those who want to and can, should.
We can do a relay strike, one group
per week so not everyone has to suffer long.
Mami raises her hand.
I will start it off.

No, Gabriela, not you. You've got a baby.
I hardly eat anyway.

No way. Who else would like to?
Listen, it will mean more because of the baby.

Marisel bites down on her lip. But then she agrees.

> *A pregnant woman*
> *on a hunger strike might be*
> *the most powerful thing.*
>> Mami! Not you. What if it isn't safe?
Amorcito, I will only do it a few days
to start it off, and then the others will help us.

Already, my heart wants
to push past my chest.

I am so scared
of what a strike
will do.

DEMANDS

Marisel turns to me.
We need a list of demands.
Betita, please give us a couple of pages
from your notebook
so we can write them out.

I clutch my notebook to my chest
when I see she's coming over
but Mami gently pulls
my hands away from it
and rips out a few pages
herself and gives Marisel
my black crayon.

They write:
> We are thirty-five mothers, caretakers, and children who have chosen to stop eating in protest of the current inhumane conditions for all detainees. We demand that our human rights, as defined by the Universal Declaration of Human Rights, be respected. As such, we demand conditions for all detainees be improved to reflect this. We demand the following:
> - Access to legal representation
> - No separation from our children under any circumstances
> - Already-separated children be returned to parents

- Moderate temperature inside the facility
- Cots or mats and real blankets
- Warm, well-cooked meals
- Access to clean water
- On-site medical care and medicine
- School supplies and instruction for our children
- More playtime or access to the outdoors
- Respectful treatment from all staff

We will continue our hunger strike until our demands are met.

Mami weaves the ends
of the notebook papers
holding our list of demands
into the fence by
tearing them a little.

She gives me an idea:
to weave toilet paper
into the links in the fence
like the ribbons in Tina's
backyard quince.
I spell:
      STRIKE
in square letters
as tall as me.

It is the strongest word
I've ever spelled.

HOW THEY LAUGHED

When the day guards
first notice the demands
they laugh like hyenas.

By the end of breakfast
the trash can is filled with
untouched terrible rotten food
and the guards laugh some more.

Then the night guards
notice, and they also hyena howl
to see the trash can fill with
more untouched terrible rotten food.

They bang on our cage
and say we are stupid
to be hurting ourselves.

Don't listen to them, gente
we cannot be deterred,
Marisel says, and waves them away
with a quick swipe
of her hand.

HOW LONG?

At the end of the first night
I can hear Mami's belly
grumble, but she looks patient
and proud.
> How long will you not eat, Mami?
Only a few days, until they notice.
They are hurting us more than
we can ever hurt ourselves.

I poke at her belly just to see
if the egg will respond
and it does right on cue
and I worry a little less.

A DIFFERENT HUNGER

I draw a picture of a line of cranes with wide-open mouths.

Cranes are hungry
to be treated
with kindness.
Betita—March 19

ON THE THIRD DAY

without eating Mami moves her
hands slowly while she tries
to catch piojos in my hair.

She lies down.
Looks weak.
Doesn't teach.

          Are you feeling okay, Mami?
I ask for the hundredth time.
I'm a little tired today, mi'ja.
She pets my head and rubs
the egg at the same time
and she lets out a little *ay.*

Yellow Hair comes over
when she hears us
and taunts,
          Getting tired, stupid? Well, if
          you keep it up, we will throw
          you in the hole for child endangerment.
          What kind of mother goes on a
          hunger strike while pregnant?
Before Mami can respond
Marisel comes straight for Yellow Hair
wraps her fingers into the fence
and spits,
What kind of treatment
is the one you are giving all of us?

Look around. You think this is justice?
You think this is humane?

> You are getting what you deserve!
> You ignorant people put yourselves
> here by breaking the laws of my country.

You think we deserve to be in a concentration camp for
seeking asylum? You have NO idea what
most of us are running from. Most of us
had no choice but to try to find a better life.

> It is simple, you break the law
> you have to pay the consequences.

What kind of demon are you? YOU
are the one who is breaking the law!
This is cruel and unusual punishment!
Marisel roars at Yellow Hair and bangs
and bangs on the fence!
YOU are breaking the law!
YOU are breaking the law!
She screams over and over again
while she rattles and rattles the cage.

Suddenly, Mami shoots up to her
feet and begins to hurry across
the floor toward the toilet
but when she is halfway there
she stops.

> A stream
> of blood comes
> flooding out
from between her legs.
> ¡No puede ser!

Mami's face is sunken in shock.
       Mami!! I run to her.
She trembles as she
holds the lower part of
her nest. She doesn't touch me.
       Help, please! I scream. Please!
Mami turns to Yellow Hair
and pleads with a look
so hurt it needs
no words.

Yellow Hair yells,
Code Red! Code Red!
to the other guards on duty.
Marisel and Josefina rush
to Mami's side to lay her down.

They open the gate
and two mean-looking guards come in
slapping on gloves. They
place a cloth between her legs.
Hold it there, they tell her.

I am so scared I can't swallow.
       ¡Mamita, mamita!
Shards of fear seize me.
Betita, it's okay, chiquita, it's okay, her voice shakes.
But it is not.
There is so much blood.
       Mami, our egg. Mami, our baby!

Then each guard grabs ahold
of Mami's arms
to try to make her walk.

But she can't.

They grunt
as they lift her
and drag
my bleeding
mami away
from
me.

DESPAIR

rips
through
my
veins
and
tears
my
heart
to
shreds.

I CRY ONE HUNDRED MILES

I don't know how
to count how much I cry.
  Is it in time?
   Is it counted in miles?
   In times tables?
It stutters
  stops
    goes forward
then backward.

I don't know if I'm
speaking a language
other than tears.

I only know the words
  Mami, Mami, Mami.

I only understand
she has been taken to a prison hospital
one hundred miles away.

SOLITA

Our cell is given
bleach and water
to clean Mami's blood
from the floor.

They work in silence
except for my crying
and our coughing
louder and raspier
because of the bleach.

The other mothers huddle
around me like I'm
an orphan crane
in the flock.

But we are not a flock
and we are not cranes.

We are the same.
Unwanted.
Unwelcomed.
Human.
Caged.

Though they
are with me
       I am
without

my mami
      I am
without
my papi.

I am
      solita
now.

WHAT YELLOW HAIR FOUND OUT

Marisel comes to sit with me
and asks Yanela, who just sits quietly
next to me, to give us a minute.
I pull my knees to my chest
and bury my head into my arms.

She begins a sentence
but then stops
and goes quiet again.
I'm sorry, kid, she finally says.
You probably blame me for
what happened to your mom, yeah?
But we both know she hasn't
been feeling well for a while.
I mean, three days of not eating
wouldn't have caused her to
bleed like that. You got to know.

Words drain from me.

Looks like Yellow Hair
grew some sympathy finally.
She told me she found out
that your mother was saved
and that the baby was delivered.
You've got a baby sister!

I pull up my head trying to grasp the dulzura
wrapped inside what she is saying.
          Alive? A sister?

Her words slow down.
But they are both very sick, kid.
We don't know if they will
pull through, especially the baby.

          Why?   Why?   WHY?

I drop my head
and hug
my knees again.
I rock myself
unable to find
the strength
to stop
the endless
falling
of my cries.

I DRAW AND SPELL IN ALAS

I draw a pool of blood.
I spell:

> Mami.
> Betita—March 20

I draw Mami handcuffed to a prison hospital bed
I spell:

> Wake up, Mami. Come back to me!
> Betita—March 21

I draw a baby in a box attached to tubes.
I spell:

> You don't have a name.
> Please let me know your face.
> Betita—March 22

I draw myself alone in a desert at night with a moon.
I spell:

> I walk in a sandstorm of moonlight and tears.
> Betita—March 23

I draw myself with a big hole in my panza.
I spell:

> What is food for
> when I am only
> hungry for Mami.
> Betita—March 24

I no longer draw cranes or wings, only a bunch of cages.
I spell:

I don't believe in flying.

Betita—March 25

IN MAMI'S OUTLINE

Josefina tries to make me eat
but I can't.

She tries to make me sleep
in my same spot near Yanela

who is more faraway lost than ever,
but I don't sleep.

I wonder if Tía Raquel knows
what happened to Mami

all the way from the other side
of this maze of cages.

I stay awake to find the outline
of Mami's space on the concrete next to me.

I count the times the guards
light up our faces with a flashlight.

When they get near, I close my eyes
pretend to be asleep.

I count ten flashing lights to the face
in one night.

I wonder how it is I slept
through that before.

I wonder how long
they'll continue the hunger strike.

I wonder if Fernanda
will ever come back.

I wonder if Papi knows
he has another daughter now.

I wonder about Mami and the baby
fighting to live.

NEW TESTIMONIES

I don't know how to look
into anyone's eyes
but the blank pages
of Alas.

Marisel comes over
to see, but I hover
over what I draw.

*Hey, kid, can I see
what you're working on?*

       No.

*Come on, I won't judge.
I just want to see.*
She tugs my sleeve.

I finally look up
at the warm breeze
of her smile and
the *I'm sorry* in her eyes
and how mad I am
at her begins to skirt away.

I plop down Alas
and open her up.

Your pieces are beautiful,
she says as she flips through the pages.
What are they called?

Crane, I mean, picture poems.
Ms. Martinez taught me.
They show your feelings.

Who are they for?

They are for Papi.
Fernanda is supposed
to get them to him.

That's really awesome of her.

Well, they're also
for the judge.
They're testimonies
for our case.

Interesting. I'm sure
they're going to be real useful.

That's if she ever
comes back for them.

She's supposed to come
soon, Betita. When she does
you'll be ready. I wish
we all had testimonies like these.
They could really help us.

Then, a spark snaps
into my
mind
and before I know it

I'm saying,

> We could all do them.
> I have plenty of paper.

Really? But, you'd have to teach us how it's done.

> That'd be the easiest.

I feel a light and airy feeling
inside to think I can
be a teacher like Mami.

HOW TO LOOK INSIDE

It isn't hard
to remember
how Ms. Martinez
taught me.
I tear thirty-five sheets
from Alas
set them out
with my crayons
show everyone
a few of mine
as samples.

      To make a picture poem
      first, close your eyes.
I tell them.
      Then let your imagination
      lead to where your heart is
      and ask,
            How are you feeling?
      Now sit with the answer
      and if it is sad or scary
      or happy or grumpy
      then ask yourself,
            What does your feeling look like?
            What shapes appear?
            What words appear?
            What story are you telling?

You don't have to use
many words or draw
a lot of details.
The two can help
each other tell
what's in your heart.
Never forget
to sign and date them
at the bottom.

This is exactly what I do
when I make one of mine.

THEY DRAW AND SPELL

A princess with a broken crown.

Papi, you told me you would bring me to the place where princesses are born.

A cargo train with people riding on top, hanging on the sides, reaching for others on the ground.

We rode La Bestia to get here. Once, some women gave us a bag of food.

Kids playing with a soccer ball in a field and men with guns spraying bullets.

I played fútbol with my friends before they came to kill us.

People riding on a raft on a river being led by a man with a coyote's face.

Coyotes are animals that howl in the night and take your money and your soul too.

Marisel draws a girl with thought-bubble swirls all around her head.

I dream of a day when all migrants are free and I am too.

Carlos draws a boxy superhero with lightning bolts for hands.

Super Electric has arrived to knock down the bad guys.

Yanela draws a girl flying over a field of flowers.

When I am a crane, no one can hurt me.

Josefina draws a woman reaching for three children on the other side of a fence.

The day they took my children, I died inside.

Ellie draws a girl standing by the seashore, holding a smaller boy's hand.

MY little brother is gone because we were too poor to buy him medicine.
He was my best friend.

Ellie's mom draws a crying woman holding a child in her arms.

If I could hold you one more time, my boy, if I could hold you.

AN OUT-OF-PAPER CAMPAIGN

We make three picture poems each
and Alas is almost out of paper
so we have to stop.

I ask Marisel if I can keep
a few sheets for myself.
Of course, kid. Maybe these
will be enough for Fernanda
to launch our campaign.

        What campaign?
        I thought they were for lawyers?
The world needs to see
these picture poems, kid.
She sits up to argue.

They go beyond hashtags.
They are telling the true story
of who we are, where we've
come from, and what we need.
        That's not what they're for, Marisel!
Probably not to you, but if you think
about it, these drawings might
be what people need to see
to understand how much we suffer.
        I don't know.
Trust me. Please, kid.
We should at least try.

I say okay because I know
picture poems have never let me down.

TIMES TABLE SONGS

Some of the kids sing their times tables
together during outdoor time.
They stopped doing it indoors
because it makes me cry
to think la escuelita goes on
without Mami.

I can hear them even though
I am on the opposite side
of the yard watching Yanela
and Ellie chase each other
around a trash can.

I don't know if I will ever
see Mami or Papi again.

I don't know if I will ever
meet my baby sister.

PAPER YELLOW AIR

She didn't say how or why
but she held a fat stack
of paper and a plastic box
filled with crayons
and put them on the floor
inside our cell.

Then she locked the gate
and left the smell of
her yellow hair
in the air
behind her.

FINALLY, FERNANDA

Fernanda can't
hold back the quiver
in her voice when she
finally speaks to me.
I don't care.

      I want my mami.
      I want my baby sister.
      I want my papi,

I say, like a recording on repeat.
I wish I could give them to you, sweetheart,
but I can't. Your mami and your sister
both still have a blood infection. Their condition is delicate.

      Why can't I be with them?
      I could help them.
      I could sing to them.

They can't be around other people and because
you have to stay here to wait with Tía Raquel.

      But I haven't even seen Tía Raquel!
I will have to look into getting you
into the same cell, in the very least.

      Why can't Papi be with Mami and the baby, then?
Because he has to stay in Mexico. I wasn't
able to get ahold of him before I came.

      But we are a family!
I scream.

      I don't get it.
      ¡No entiendo, no entiendo!
foams from my mouth.

I don't understand
and Fernanda
can't do
a thing.

MARISEL'S FERNANDA

Marisel paces in front of me
when she's done with Fernanda.
I gave her
almost one hundred
of our picture poems
for the campaign.
           Twenty-five of those
           are some of my best.
You're our teacher, they ARE the best!

The group she works with
is going to do an art exhibit
and they'll hang them up and
invite people, newspeople too.

           Do you think they will hang them
           on a laundry line
           like Mami used to do with mine?

Marisel moves one strand of hair
behind my ear as she says,
They'll probably put them in frames, kid,
to sell them to raise money to pay Fernanda
so she can keep working for us for free.

That's something I never thought
about. Marisel knows
another side of Fernanda
I don't even know.

I COUNT

twenty days since Mami bled
twenty sunlight times
twenty more moms and kids
inside our cell crying
their hands, lips, and feet
turning cold blue.
Twenty more times I don't
want to fly with Yanela and Ellie
or fight with Carlos.
Even baby Jakie doesn't
make me laugh.

I count one kick in my face
while I slept, from a guard
who was looking for
someone else.

And fifteen days since
Fernanda took our picture poems
but now she is back
to tell us
　　　　our campaign is starting to go viral!
AND, people are protesting because
they saw the pictures and words
of our nightmares
and it scared them too.

REQUEST

Marisel and I
get called to the office
without a warning.
       Marisel, what if we're in trouble
       because of the picture poems?
She rubs the top of my hand before
she holds it and pulls me to walk.
I wouldn't put it past them. They suck.

We are taken to an empty room
except for a few chairs and
a bunch of equipment
I've never seen.

There are a couple of fancy clothes
there with Fernanda
who aren't lawyers but who say
they are reporters.
*We would like to talk to you both
if that is okay?*

I pull Marisel's hand away,
but she pulls me back.
       I can't. I don't want to.
*Listen, Betita, this might
be the only way to get us out
of here. Maybe someone will
see this and help us.*

A woman reporter interrupts,
You don't need to worry
we can only capture your silhouette
because you are a minor.

So I slowly sit with Marisel
in front of big lights
big cameras
in a big room
to talk about
the hunger strike
and our
picture poems
and what we've
been through.

HOPE LIKE A FALLEN SKY

When we tell the others about the interview
Josefina asks us to pray to be set free.
She says maybe this will be it.
I close my eyes and don't pray.
All my wishes are strangled
inside a fallen sky
that only knows
this cement floor
these fences
the no-nothings that can be dones
the blood infection baby sisters and Mamis
the faraway Papis
the you stay theres
the solitas
the hunger strikes
the viral picture poems
the Alas
with only four of my own pages
left to feel and spell
with only four
pages left
of sky
to fall
into.

WHEN THE GOVERNMENT COMES

They are a swarm
of uniforms and suits
like a mess of wild wasps
attacking.

They are rude when
they break up our cell.
Children cry and cling to mothers
when they make a line of adults
and begin to place a thick electronic brace
on their ankles, tightly.
Anklets that mean some sort of freedom?
Marisel says these braces will track them
so they show up to court
but first they have to pay a small bail bond.

Marisel is called into that line
she begins to light up with happiness
like the others, no matter that
the suits wear scowls and stiff eyes.

Other families are lined up and told
they will be transferred
to a temporary family housing shelter
run by a charity, with beds,
fresh clothes, no cages
and they will be
together.

Yanela, Carlos, and Jackie
line up next to Josefina with
smiles so bright they shine.

Josefina doesn't get out of line
but blows me handfuls of kisses
then lifts
            her arms in front of her
                        and makes them round
                        as if her air hug
            could reach
me.

Yanela pulls free
                        and runs to my side.
She holds both my hands
says, *Cuídate mucho, Betita*
as she wraps me in a hug.
Thank you for being my only
friend. Thank you for teaching me to fly.
            You take good care too, Yanela.
I hold on to her extra long
before she breaks away and joins
the line, waving.

Parents still waiting for their
children to be returned will
stay in an adult cell until
they can make a connection
with their kids
their faces torn
with sadness.

The almost solitas and their kids
who have someone
waiting for them on the
outside will be released.

Suddenly, I see a face I think
I recognize walk through the gate.
My Tía Raquel has come
into the cage with me!
        But she is not the same.
Her eyes are two sunken holes,
her face is so thin her cheekbones
look like sharp razor blades,
her lips are as cracked
as old pavement,
and she doesn't speak.
        Tía, it's me, Betita! I say.
She doesn't respond
but looks right through me
like a person eaten by despair.

I will stay right here
inside this monster
with childless parents
and parentless children
        like me.

WE DID SOMETHING

Marisel mouths words
to me I can't make
out at first. She moves
farther away in line.
I think she says,
Thank you, kid! You did this! Thank you!
But I can't be sure.

We *did* do something.

I put Alas to my chest
take a deep breath
and smile
feeling my heart
tug with happiness
for them and
collapse with
an ache as big as
a mountain
for my family
too.

A MEXICAN GIFT

I have no update to give you, Betita.
I haven't been able to get in touch
with anyone with a brain
at the prison hospital.
Fernanda is calmly worried.
      I know.
You should feel so proud for making
things really change here, Betita.
      Yeah.
Your picture poems have gone
across the country and have helped
so many people understand.
      They were everyone's work.
      But they didn't help me.
That's because I can't ask for a court date
until I know your mother's condition.
But once I do and we show the judge
your drawings, I have a good feeling
you will be able to get asylum.
I shrug because I don't believe her, but I don't say so.

I have some things for you, Betita.
A new notebook with better paper
and some new crayons.
      Thank you, Fernanda, I say,
      my seriousness
      swallowing
      the truth of what I really want.

And this envelope here
is from your father, in Mexico.
          Papi?
Yes, sweetheart, your papi.
It has been opened because
it needed to pass inspection.

A guard hands me Fernanda's gifts.
                    My hands shake
                              as I reach for the envelope
                    and begin to open it
          so slowly
my palms sweat.
          When I lift the flap
                    I can smell Papi again!
                              The smell of him is mixed
                    with the scent of plants and earth
          I don't recognize.
But I close the lid and ask,
          Can I take these?
Absolutely!

I thank her and
say goodbye so quickly
I trip over my words.

MI QUERIDA BETITA PLUMITA,
MY LITTLE CRANE,

I hope that when you read this letter, we are one day closer to being together again. It is so difficult to try to explain to you why we are apart. I have trouble understanding it myself. I have been so worried, amorcito, because Mami and the baby are so sick, and worried you are all alone in that place. I don't know how things got so mixed up. I don't know how this will all turn out. All I can say is, I'm sorry. I am so, so sorry, Betita. I hope one day you will find a way to understand and to forgive me.

Fernanda tells me how brave you have been and about how you taught people to fly into the beauty of their suffering, like I've always reminded you to do and how that has changed things for so many. You've always been so good at flying.

I am especially grateful for the crane poems you sent me. I don't know which one is my favorite. Each one made my heart soar, made me feel so close to you, but also, some made me cry because I cannot believe how much you have been through and I wished to be there. Flying together. Because you do, you fly like a tocuilcoyotl, inside these poems and pictures, even if you think your wings are gone.

I have tried to write crane poems to you too. Some were not so good, so I only included the best ones here. The ones with más sentimiento, like you do it. I tried, I really did. When I see you again, I will have to be a better student.

Before I end this letter, I want you to take something straight into the center of your bones. You are the daughter and granddaughter of people who work hard at all things. We work hard to love, to live a decent life, to be and do good, to be one of the many cranes that migrate, searching for a safe home. Please don't ever forget that. Please don't ever forget you come from this flight for freedom.

I love you from here to where the stars never end.

Amor eterno,
Tu Papi

PAPI POEMS

He drew a flock of cranes flying over a big wall.
He spelled:

> We are cranes.
> Though we are apart
> one day we will fly together again
> to find Aztlán waiting.

He drew my face surrounded by clouds.
He spelled:

> Across a reddish-blue sky
> I see you in the
> wind-swept clouds
> and I miss you.

He drew a crane landing in an agave field.
He spelled:

> You have been in my work
> earth
> rain
> hands
> sorrow
> dreams
> struggle
> healing
> heart
> skin
> You have been in my wings.

WINGED WORDS

Through pages of love
I read to learn I've always
known how to fly free.

I FIND A SPACE

near silent Tía Raquel
in the cage for
my silver blanket
and my new mat
inside the same cold
the same piojos
the same toilet
the same fear
of all us cranes
with tearstained cheeks
and faraway faces
left
waiting.

I give them paper.
I give them what I know.
I tell them
right here is a
way to take to the
sky or to make
it bend into
your heart
so it
flies.

At least the heart.
At least that.

CYCLONE DUST

When I get called to the
office again, they tell me
to bring my things.
> Alas I and II, my crayons,
> Papi's letter, and crane poems.

They give me a plastic bag
with the things they took
from Mami and me.
> Her handbag plus
> fifty cents for chocolate milk
> a shiny concrete rock that glimmers in the sun
> and a folded crane poem for Papi
> I made at school so long ago.
> The dried dead bee I collected in the yarda
> is now dust, just dust.

You're being processed for deportation.
> Deportation? Where?
*To Guadalajara, Mexico. Your relative Roberto Quintero
will be there to receive you.*
> But what about Mami? What about the baby?
I pound my closed fist on the table.
> I will not leave here without them!
I am empty of tears. Nothing but anger fills up my voice.

*Settle down! They're in the holding cell across the hall.
You'll be traveling with them.*
> What?

What he said
wrecks my head
like a cyclone
making landfall.

A SILENCE

At first
        I don't have breath, or sight.
I don't have a sentence, or a picture.
        I reach to find
            a silence beyond my body.
It doesn't recognize the woman
        hugging me, it doesn't
            know her voice, her choking cry,
Mi niña, mi niña. Betita, I'm here.

        It doesn't recognize
            the sweet pattern of her face
but somehow, somehow
        I find a glimmer that
encourages me to smile.
I find an opening where
        memories float
back into me
to the longing for
        the Mami I wanted
            so much I called for
            her in my sleep
        the Mami I imagined in
        a grave of flowers
        I would never see.

That Mami is
now sweeping large
golden-brown wings

around my own
so tightly I
want to fold
into them
and let my
disbelief go and
allow all of her love
to hold me.

THE EGG HAS A NAME

Mami opens a lumpy cloth
wrapped across her chest.

I don't believe what
I see
a baby crane
with little feathery ears
rounded lips
like a puckered beak
sleeping.

This is your baby sister, mi'ja.
Her name is Alba.
          Alba?
It means the first light of day.

I give her the lightest
kiss on her little head
but don't get too close
so she doesn't
catch my piojos
or my cough.

Her name is a drizzle
in my mind where I imagine
a crane poem for her
          a horizon with only the top of a sun with eyes, peeking.

Alba, a crane who moves
from the night
and enters the light.

THE MOUNTAIN BEFORE US

Mami, why are they sending us to Mexico
where the men might find us?
Where they might find Papi?
I am so afraid of the mountain, Mami.
They are sending us because I asked them to.
It is called "voluntary departure."
Why would you? What about Fernanda
and our case for asylum—to be safe?
My heart and body are broken, amor,
she says, and cups her hand over my face.
We have all suffered so much. Now that I have you
I can't bear for us to continue to live like this.
We need to be together again. We need to be juntos
even though I am afraid of Mexico too.
But I don't remember Mexico.
I remember East LA.
My school.
Our yarda.
Will we ever come back?
We are cranes meant to migrate, right?
It is possible we might
one day, we might.

A MECHANICAL CRANE

Higher above the land
than I have ever flown
                closer to the sun
all below fades
        from buildings and brush
to deserts
        into an ocean of clouds.

I feel Papi's words
        curl their way
into my arms.
        Dulzura, struggle, beauty
and they are mine too.
        Mami and baby Alba
beside me.
        Cranes in flight.

Soon, Papi's
waiting eyes
        will meet ours
in the warmest hugs again
        he will see Alba fly
for the first time
        and all those days
without one another
        will swirl into a mist
that forgives
        a wind that is love

to help us face
    the thunder of danger, together.

                Soon, we will
            bring in our wings
        and touch the earth
of another home.

Dear Reader,

Thank you for your courage to bear witness to Betita's difficult story. While this is a work of fiction, much of what is shared is based on the experiences of real migrant children and their families. Her story is one that can be folded into a larger tragic and true story of the criminalization of migration that spans hundreds of years in the United States.

The history of humanity across the globe is one of migration. The Americas were populated just this way. We know of Aztlán, one of the homelands of the Mexica people (the place Betita's father, Beto, references in the myth), because it was a migration story told through the Codex Boturini (one of the few remaining books of precolonial Mesoamerica). On the surface, the reasons why we migrate are too vastly different to see any commonality. However, when we look closely, the need to migrate is very similar in both the human and animal worlds. If we look at migration patterns—not only of people, but of cranes and other species—we will notice what all migrants have in common: They migrate to survive changes to their environment and for their well-being. It is humans who have drawn the lines in the sand, erected walls and borders around their territories, and deemed people "illegal" when they cross those walls and borders.

The Trump administration's "zero tolerance" policy saw thousands of migrant children, mostly Central American, separated from their parents, kept in cages, and treated inhumanely. This policy also brought about an increase in the number of migrants who died trying to cross the border or while in custody. Despite worldwide protest over the clear violations of human rights, this administration continues to hurt asylum-seeking children and families as its laws change for the worse each day to our continued horror. There is no compassion when migrants arrive, nor is there understanding for the reasons people are forced to flee their homelands with their children. I am heartbroken and appalled, not only by the Trump administration or previous administrations, but also by everyday citizens who support the message of hate toward migrants. Their hateful views and their entitled claims to land and territory disregard the First Nations of the United States, hundreds of years of migration, and really, the human suffering that is at the very root of why people migrate.

I wrote *Land of the Cranes* with an understanding of the long and devastating history of raids, separations, deportations, incarcerations, and deaths my community has suffered. But also, I wrote from an intimate place. I, like

Betita, was an undocumented child. I was born in Mexico and brought to the United States as a baby. My childhood fear of "La Migra" (immigration enforcement) and how they could easily rip our family apart hung over me until we received our green cards, though this was not necessarily a guarantee of safety. The immigrant community in which Betita was raised in East LA, and the fears, stigmas, and prejudices her community faced are mine, too. Though I was never detained or deported for being a migrant, some in my family and many in my community have been. This is a story I had to tell for us. But this is not the *only* story. This book is part of a wider literary tradition by numerous authors who've been speaking to the wound of migration for many generations.

I chose to name some of the characters in the book after children who died while in detention or while migrating. I did so with the utmost respect and love and also in order to honor their memory and add resonance to their lives—even if only within the pages of this book. I am hopeful more stories from the Central American perspective will rise to speak to the deep tragedies and sufferings they have endured. Their stories need to be told, especially because these communities—many of which are indigenous—make up the largest groups of migrants coming to the border today.

While these injustices may seem impossible to challenge, this crisis requires we break open our own humanity to try to find positive solutions. Our solutions must be steeped in respect for migrants and for their heart-breaking circumstances, and those solutions cannot be achieved by building more walls nor by acting with cruelty. I believe in our collective loving spirit, and this book, this long picture poem, is my offering de esperanza.

Thank you for taking the journey with Betita. May you, like her, search to find light in your darkest hour, or as her Papi says, "find sweetness in your struggle." May you see that as a child, like Betita, you have the power to write, to draw, to speak up against and shut down the forces that seek to make migrants criminals. May your wings, your voice, help us, members of the human family, rise above the hate and carry the much-needed compassion and justice for migrants into a vast migration of change across the globe. All of us with love, flying, together.

Acknowledgments

Immeasurable gratitude to my beloved mamá, Maria Isabel Viramontes Salazar, whose winged love always carried me. Thank you, Mami, for your gorgeous life—immigrant and dream-filled, joyful and strong, patient and faithful, truthful and giving, and always basked in tender and unconditional amor. My world will never be the same without you. Que sueñes con los angelitos.

My precious loves, John, Avelina, and João, thank you for teaching me the profound work of growing wings of my own. To my great big immigrant family—Papi, brother, sisters, nieces, nephews, in-laws, tías, tíos, and cousins, wounded as we are and as we've been by life and loss, I love you and thank you for everything.

Muchas gracias to Las Musas and to the Xingona Collective, your fire and your Latina word wisdom make my soul and writing strive to reach new heights. Special thanks to my dear friends and colleagues in the literary world, in my community, and in my close circle. Gracias for giving me important feedback and support, then ample space and love, while I re-wrote this book and cared for and then grieved for Mami. Les quiero con el alma.

Marietta Zacker, incomparable agent and amiga del corazón, gracias for being a pillow, a backbone, a bridge, a mirror, a springboard, a visionary, and a chola in all the best ways.

Nick Thomas, my deepest gratitude for believing in the importance of this story from the start, for your intelligence and remarkable generosity in editing this manuscript and for urging me to make Betita's voice sing. Thank you Andrea Davis Pinkney and Jess Harold for picking up the baton with so much care and running with me to the finish line. To the phenomenal team at Scholastic: Lizette Serrano, Daniel Yadao, Emily Heddleson, Sydney Tillman, Amy Goppert,

Melissa Schirmer, Rachel Feld, Julia Eisler, Lauren Donovan, Maria Dominguez, Ellie Berger, Dick Robinson, the biggest hearts in the biz, thank you for opening so many doors and for supporting my work with an unwavering spirit. Magical book designer, Maeve Norton, and cover and illustration artists, Quang & Lien, thank you for working so hard to make this book more beautiful than I could have ever imagined.

My greatest respect and appreciation to immigration journalists, Tina Vasquez, Aura Bogado, and Roberto Lovato and immigration attorney, Fernanda Bustamante. Your work as Latinx folks documenting the migrant experience with dignity and being in the trenches fighting for immigrant rights have been a tremendous gift. This book walks in your light. Thanks also to Lily and Zoe Ellis, and Kaia Marbin, your "Butterfly Effect: Migration is Beautiful" nationwide art project to make 75,000 (and counting) paper butterflies in honor of every child held in detention is such an incredible example of how art can make a change.

Special praise for the activists, the fighters, the peacemakers, the resisters, the writers, the artists, and the dreamers standing up for justice and truth. Thank you for your struggle to make the world a better place. Onward!

My most heartbroken love for Jakelin Caal Maquin (age 7), Felipe Gómez Alonzo (age 8), Wilmer Josué Ramírez Vásquez (age 2), Carlos Hernandez Vasquez (age 16), Mariee Juárez (age 20 months), Darlyn Cristabel Cordova-Valle (age 10), and Juan de León Gutiérrez (age 17), who lost their young lives while in immigration custody and to the unnamed migrant children who have also died while incarcerated or while crossing the border, to those separated from their parents, to those who have been or remain incarcerated and endure(d) the brutality of that experience. You matter, and I am so sorry.

AFTER WORDS™

AIDA SALAZAR'S
Land of the Cranes

CONTENTS

After Words™ guide by Jennifer Thompson

About the Author

Aida Salazar is an award-winning author and arts activist whose writings explore issues of identity and social justice. She was born in Mexico and grew up in a family of seven children in Southeast Los Angeles. This is where she spent many days sitting in little puddles of water on cement believing she was in the ocean.

Her critically acclaimed and award-winning debut middle-grade novel in verse, *The Moon Within*, has been hailed as "important" by the *New York Times*; as "a worthy successor to *Are You There God? It's Me Margaret*" by *Kirkus Reviews*; as "revolutionary and culturally ecstatic" by Juan Felipe Herrera (US Poet Laureate); won an International Latino Book Award for Middle Grade Fiction, a Golden Poppy Award, a Nerdy Book Award, an Américas Award Honor, an NCTE Notable Poetry and Verse Novel Award; and was named a Charlotte Huck Recommended Book by NCTE. It received four starred reviews from *School Library Journal*, *Kirkus Reviews*, *Publishers Weekly* and *BookPage*; was named a best book of 2019 by NPR's Book Concierge, *Kirkus Reviews*, *School Library Journal*, New York Public Library, The Center for Multicultural Children's Literature, and Penn State Graduate School of Education; and a best book of the decade by Ellen Hagan for *School Library Journal*. It was featured on NPR's *Weekend Edition*, KPFA's *Hard Knock Radio*, on *Making Contact*, and the *Feeling My Flow* podcast. *The Moon Within* was printed in paperback as part of Scholastic's exclusive Gold line of award-winning books and has been translated into Spanish by Alberto Jiménez Rioja.

Land of the Cranes won the Américas Award; a California Librarian's Association John and Patricia Beatty Award; a Northern California Book Award; the NCTE Charlotte Huck Award Honor; and a Jane Addams Peace Award Honor. It is an International Latino Book Award silver medalist, and a Rhode Island Book Award finalist; it was selected as 2021–2022 Project LIT Book Club Pick; and chosen as a Rise Feminist Book by the American Library Association. *Land of the Cranes* has also gained starred reviews from *Kirkus Reviews* who called it "powerful . . . lyrical . . . soaring . . ." from *Publishers Weekly* who called it "lyrical, passionate, and all-too timely," and a star from *School Library Journal*, who called it "beautifully told, heart-wrenching and resonant." It was named a Best Book of the Year by *Kirkus Reviews*, *School Library Journal*, *BookPage*, and The Center for Multicultural Children's Books, and was named one of the top ten books of the year by the New York Public Library. It was a BookCon 2020 Middle Grade Buzz Book and was featured on the BBC's World Service's program *The Cultural Frontline*. *Land of the Cranes* was translated into Spanish by Abel Berriz.

Her picture book, based on the life of her distant great aunt, Jovita Valdovinos, *Jovita Wore Pants: The Story of A Mexican Freedom Fighter*, is illustrated by Molly Mendoza. She wrote the poems for an anthology created by Alina Chau, entitled In *The Spirit of A Dream: 13 Stories of American Immigrants of Color*. She is co-editing *Calling the Moon: Period Stories by BIPOC Authors* with Yamile Saied Méndez. Her forthcoming historical fiction novel, *A Seed In The Sun*, about a farm-working girl who longs to be a teatrista and is inspired by Dolores Huerta during the pivotal moments of the 1965

UFW grape boycott, is set to be published in 2022 by Dial Books for Young Readers. Her work has appeared in the middle-grade anthology *This Is Our Rainbow*, and the young adult anthologies *Living Beyond Borders* and *Allies*. She has translated two picture books from English into Spanish: *Paz (Peace)* written by Baptiste and Miranda Paul and illustrated by Estelí Meza; and *Ojala Supieras (I Wish You Knew)* written by Jackie Azua Kramer and illustrated by Magdalena Mora. She has also translated into English the novel *Neverforgotten (Nuncaseolvida)*, written by Alejandra Algorta and illustrated by Ivan Rickenmann. Her story *By the Light of the Moon* was adapted into a ballet production by choreographer Isabelle Sjahsam and artist Roberto Miguel for the Sonoma Conservatory of Dance, and premiered in April 2016. It is the first Xicana-themed ballet in history.

With an MFA in writing from the California Institute of the Arts, Aida's work for adults has appeared in publications such as the *Huffington Post*, *Huizache Magazine*, *Voices of Our Ancestors: Xicanx and Latinx Spiritual and Healing Practices*, *Latina Struggles and Protest in the 21st Century USA*, and *Women and Performance: Journal of Feminist Theory*. She is a founding member of Las Musas, the first collective of Latinx kidlit authors in US children's literature. She is also a co-founder of Latinx Luna, a collective challenging menstruation stigmas in Latinx communities.

Aida lives with her family of artists in a teal house in Oakland, CA.

Children's Plus Interview

This interview was first released as a video interview between book distributor Children's Plus and Aida Salazar. Enjoy this first-ever print version!

Hello, I am Aida Salazar, author of the middle grade novel, *Land of the Cranes* and *The Moon Within*.

Q: *Can you tell us more about the inspiration and story behind the crane and how it is woven throughout Betita's story?*
A: The metaphor of the crane comes from the Aztec myth Betita's father tells her. He says their people came from a place called Aztlán. which translates in English to Land of the Cranes. He said their people left Aztlán and traveled south and went to found their great city in the navel of the universe in México-Tenochtitlan. He tells her the reason why they left Mexico is because they are like birds who have come back home to live among the cranes. So she believes she is a bird. I used the crane as a metaphor for the freedom to migrate. I used it as a way to point to the outrageousness of caging humans and children, migrants, who are seeking help, and especially ones as young as Betita. She believes she is a bird so deeply she doesn't understand why she and her family are not able to fly free like cranes and all migrating animals.

I was inspired to write Betita's story as a response to the criminalization and incarceration of migrants in the United States. There is a long history of deportations and abuses against the migrant community, which is also my community. I was undocumented until I was thirteen years old. Though I am now a US citizen, my experience and my ties to the wounds of my community make it so that I cannot look away. I wrote this story to inspire others to also not look away.

Q: *Both of your books are novels in verse, can you tell us more about the writing process?*

A: I wrote both *Land of the Cranes* as well as my first novel *The Moon Within* in verse because I am poet. Writing a story through a series of poems comes very naturally to me. Poetry gives us space and time for introspection and time to be inspired. Especially when it is written like these two books in a very close first-person perspective. We gain access to their emotions; that opens up the story in rich ways. I wanted to be gentle with my readers, I wanted them to be able to spend time with a very difficult subject, and in the case of *Land of the Cranes* I wanted them to go inside and think about the metaphors of the crane and caging, I wanted them to pause in the quietness and the figurative language that poetry offers. I chose for Betita to write picture poems because I wanted her to be a poet but also because I wanted her to know what it is to have the power to change things for the better through her art and through her voice.

Q: *How difficult was it explaining such a complicated issue through a child's eyes?*

A: Often, children have very strong moral compasses. They are often the first to point out injustice. My hope was to dive deep into this sensibility, to connect with them through Betita's sweet personality, through her language, through her confusion, through her belief in a better world for her family and for others. I allowed her story to guide me and hopefully readers will respond to that honesty.

Q: *Are there any additional resources, charities, or ways to help that you recommend to readers to help assist people like Betita and her family?*
A: Al Otro Lado, Raices Texas, Kids in Need of Defense. Write, draw, express yourself, do what you can to raise awareness about the tragedy we are living. It all helps.

Q: *Where does your courage and inspiration come from to write such important stories?*
A: I've been fighting for social justice in one way or another for over twenty-five years. The courage to write comes from a deep place of love. It hurts me to see injustice in the world. I use my writing as a tool to shine a light on it, to speak against it, and to help heal the wounds it creates. For inspiration, I need to look no further than my life, my community, and the humanity that connects us all. I wrote *Land of the Cranes* for them, for us, and for you.

Reading Guide
Land of the Cranes

Preparing Our Learning Space:

Real-world issues like family separation, racist immigration policies, and inhumane conditions must be addressed if we are to learn and do better as educators and humans. The stories of Betita and the other children and mothers in *Land of the Cranes* have given us lifelong lessons on how to discuss these topics with children. As we prepare to read and process with young learners, we must consider:

SAFETY: What are the support systems in the learning community for children to process the reality of family separation and the injustice at detention facilities? How can we create space for children to share their feelings and not feel that this is mandatory, especially for children who have experienced trauma? For example, can we partner with counselors or social workers? We can also work with colleagues to consider interdisciplinary opportunities, not only with content areas such as social studies and language arts but also with art, music, and health.

DISCUSSION ENTRY POINTS: What are the picture books, films, documentaries, artwork, songs, poems, and other media on these topics that we can engage with prior to our reading? We can read

Angela Cervantes, or *Wishes* by Mượn Thị Văn. We can use illustrations by Victo Ngai, or from *In the Spirit of a Dream*. I would pair it with the short film *Free Like The Birds* by Paola Mendoza, and the song "Ice El Hielo" by La Santa Cecilia.

TEXT SETS: Create text sets that are multimodal, and that not only reveal the horrors of this topic but also teach about resistance, advocacy, and efforts for social justice. You might include information from organizations that provide legal services, education, and community organizing, including: CASA, Al Otro Lado, Make the Road New York, and Immigration Advocates Network.

Discussion Questions

1. We learn about Aztlán and its importance in the stories that Papi shares in "Where We Land." Why is it important for Betita to know these old stories about where their family comes from and where they are going? What other stories do you know that describe the origins of a group of people and their purpose? How are these stories similar? How are they different?

2. In "Crane Poem Gallery," Betita describes Papi's way of speaking as "Spanish-sounding English warm soft round words." She notes that the principal tried to correct Betita's own "singsong East LA English," while her teacher Ms. Mar-

tinez "never cared one speck about" the way she spoke. Consider the different sounds, words, idioms, and expressions that you've heard in one or more languages. How do people react to different kinds of English and Spanish? Why do you think someone might react like the principal, as opposed to the teacher's more welcoming approach?

3. When the injustices of our world seem too heavy to carry alone, we turn to various people, places, and practices to help sustain us. In "We Planted Roses Too" and "Virgencita Angel," we witness Mami's spiritual practice. Betita says that Mami "prays for protection," and also shares more about Tio Pedro. What are some practices that help you find the support you need so you don't carry the weight of everything on your own? Where did we learn about these practices or rituals? What are other ways we can process and help one another?

4. What makes a place a "sanctuary" for immigrants? Why are these places necessary? Read the poem "Sanctuary Breakfast" and research sanctuary states. Return to the poem and consider how Papi explains the concept to Betita, saying that it is for people who get caught "wanting to fly."

5. In "The Amparo Globe" we get to know Amparo, Betita's best friend. Betita is thrilled that her friend listens to Papi's stories and "knows she is a crane too." Being thoughtful and being a careful listener are important to a strong friendship. What are some other keys to being a good friend?

6. Over the course of the book, Betita navigates some of the realities of being undocumented in the modern-day United States. In "Walls," Mami talks about the family being undocumented. In "Questions" and "Learning Tears," Betita's school facilitates a dialogue about what is happening with Immigration and Customs Enforcement (ICE) "round ups," including providing instructions to make a family plan, and social workers are present in the school, encouraging students to process these events in whatever way they'd like. In "Our Flock," the family is in conversation with lawyers when Betita learns that "Papi will be put on a plane and flown to Mexico." Consider: where, and how, do you learn about immigration issues? How do classrooms, libraries, and community events engage with these issues? What dominant narratives about immigration must we unlearn? Where do these ideas come from, and how do they compare with the counternarratives that we learn through Betita's story?

7. "No matter how we struggle, remember to keep life sweet," says Papi. What are some examples of Betita and her family finding joy in the midst of injustice? How do you and your family find joy amidst injustice in your own life?

8. Consider the physical and psychological conditions of the detention facility. How do these conditions impact the children and their mothers? Describe how Betita and Mami keep "searching for light" in the midst of the inhumane and terrifying conditions at the detention center.

9. When Betita and Mami arrive at the detention center, they meet other children and mothers that have been detained and separated from the rest of their families. What do we learn about Josefina's family and about "practically unaccompanied minors"?

10. In "Inside My Alas," "I Draw and Spell in Alas," and "They Draw and Spell," we learn more about what Betita and the other children experience in the detention facility, and about their journeys leading up to that moment. The children draw and write their feelings, experiences, and dreams. Compare their testimonies to those displayed in the University of Texas at El Paso exhibition *Uncaged Art: Tornillo Children's Detention Camp*. How did the children in the book and at the Tornillo Detention Camp use art to process?

About the Writer of this Guide

Dr. Carla España is a Bilingual/TESOL instructor at Bank Street Graduate School of Education and the co-author of *En Comunidad: Lessons for Centering the Voices and Experiences of Bilingual Latinx Students*. Her work lives at the intersection of children's literature, bilingual education, translanguaging, culturally sustaining pedagogy, and teacher preparation.

**Turn the page to enjoy
a special excerpt from
In the Spirit of a Dream
by award-winning
author Aida Salazar!**

In the Spirit of a Dream

We set out across
    continents,
    oceans,
    and borders,
to find a place where we have been told
our dreams can be made — the United States of America.

We come
as migrants, often unwanted,
to this country that will always belong
to the first nations to inhabit it,
was built largely by
those enslaved and forced here,
together with those
who are immigrants, like us.

We follow a dream
that doesn't always come true.
Sometimes, it fades before us
yet we persist and pursue it
to awaken a future of our own.

These are some of our stories,
the songs of our spirits,
our longings,
the challenges, and the heights
to which we have risen
in search of fulfilling
our wildest imaginations.

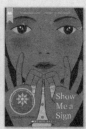